"Thanks for the invitation, but...no."

A look of mild surprise flashed across his face as if he were not accustomed to women rejecting him. "Are you going to tell me why not?" he demanded.

"I have no desire to act as a stand-in. Why this sudden interest in me, Jarvis?" Gina asked bluntly.

"My interest might have been around much sooner if you hadn't gone into hiding these past two years," he mocked her. "Now that we've met again I've no intention of letting you escape. You're going to be mine, Georgina."

"I'll never be yours," she said, spitting out the words.

"In the near future I'll prove those words a lie," he warned. "And remember, Georgina, I don't fumble when I make love to a woman."

Her breath locked in her throat. If he had intended to shock her, then he had succeeded.

YVONNE WHITTAL, a born dreamer, started scribbling stories at an early age, but admits she's glad she didn't have to make her living by writing then. "Otherwise," she says, "I would surely have starved!" After her marriage and the birth of three daughters, she began submitting short stories to publishers. Now she derives great satisfaction from writing full-length books. The characters become part of Yvonne's life in the process, so much so that she almost hates coming to the end of each manuscript and having to say farewell to dear and trusted friends.

Books by Yvonne Whittal

YVONNE WHITTAL

eldorado

Harlequin Books

TORONTO • NEW YORK • LONDON
AMSTERDAM • PARIS • SYDNEY • HAMBURG
STOCKHOLM • ATHENS • TOKYO • MILAN

Harlequin Presents first edition December 1987
ISBN 0-373-11038-3

Original hardcover edition published in 1987
by Mills & Boon Limited

CHAPTER ONE

'IT's time you found yourself a husband, my dear.'

Georgina Osborne's green eyes sparkled with amusement, and she crossed one long, shapely leg over the other as she faced the grey-haired woman seated in the chair close to hers. What had prompted that particular remark? she wondered humorously, but her humour waned as she continued to study the older woman. Evelyn Cain was in her late sixties, but she had aged visibly in recent months, and Gina's concern for her godmother escalated sharply.

'I'm not ready for marriage and the responsibilities that accompany it, Aunt Evelyn,' Gina responded, her voice attractively husky, and a smile plucking once again at the corners of her wide, soft mouth.

'When is one ever ready?' her godmother protested, raising her eyes briefly towards the beamed ceiling in Eldorado's gracious living-room while her hands gestured expressively against the mohair blanket covering her legs. 'Some man will come along one day, he'll sweep you off your feet, and suddenly you're married . . . regardless of the responsibilities.

'I guess you're right,' Gina sighed, leaning back in her chair and allowing her appreciative glance to rest for a moment on the antiques and priceless porcelain ornaments surrounding her. But her mind was not on what she was looking at.

She was thinking of Norman Thrope with his rugged good looks and calm, gentle nature. He was senior accountant at the firm of Becketts Engineering where Gina was a computer systems analyst. They had met two years ago when she had joined the company, but he had most certainly made no attempt to sweep her off her feet and into marriage, and neither had she wanted him to. They were friends, friends who shared an interest in the theatre, music, and the outdoors, and they enjoyed each other's company.

'Is there a man in your life at this moment, Gina?'

Evelyn's query sliced into Gina's thoughts, and for a startled second she wondered if the older woman had been capable of reading her mind.

'Yes and no,' Gina answered cautiously, and her godmother gestured impatiently with her thin, bony hands.

'Don't be evasive, child!'

'Yes, there is a man,' Gina admitted reluctantly, brushing back a heavy strand of red-gold hair which had fallen forward across one shoulder, 'and he's a good friend and companion.'

Evelyn Cain's grey eyes observed Gina intently, and with a strange anxiety in their depths. 'How long have you know this man?'

'Two years.'

'If, after two years, he's still merely a good friend and companion, then he's obviously not the right man for you. Imagine!' Evelyn snorted disparagingly. 'Two years!'

'It's a comfortable relationship,' Gina argued softly.

'Who wants comfort?' her godmother exploded. 'It's passion that counts, and it's passion that puts fire in your blood . . . not comfort!'

'I don't think I'm capable of that *grande passion* you're talking about,' Gina replied, colouring with embarrassment.

'Nonsense! Of course you are!' Evelyn's grey eyes were almost feverishly intent as she studied Gina's delicate features with the finely arched brows and small, straight nose. 'Why have you never told me about this man?'

'Oh, I don't know.' Gina felt vaguely unnerved, and she shifted uncomfortably in the carved satinwood armchair that dated back to the Elizabethan era. 'Perhaps I didn't think of telling you about him since there's nothing really to tell, except that we're friends and that we go out together occasionally.'

'Hmph!' The wrinkled features settled into a grim mask. 'I was hoping I would live long enough to see you safely married.'

'Of course you're going to live long enough!'

'No, Gina.' Evelyn shook her grey head, striking fear into Gina's heart. 'There's no sense whatsoever in ignoring the fact that I've got a heart that is becoming too tired lately to function.'

'I wish you wouldn't say things like that!' Gina protested, frowning, the husky quality in her voice deepening with concern.

'I must, my dear,' her godmother sighed from her reclining position in the comfortable wing-backed chair, and her features were grave in the soft light of the porcelain table lamp beside her. 'My time is limited, and although I have so much to be grateful for, there are certain things that I regret most deeply.'

Their conversation was interrupted when a maid entered the living-room with a tray of tea and, as always, placed it on the low table close to Gina.

These Friday evenings with Evelyn Cain had become a pleasing ritual during the two years since Gina had come to live and work in Johannesburg. She would drive out to Houghton when she left the office on Fridays and stay until after dinner in this magnificent old house, with its history that dated back to 1905. Her pleasure on that particular evening was, however, tainted by an icy fear that was beginning to gnaw away at her.

'Shall I pour?' Gina asked quietly, aware of the need to occupy herself in some way.

'Please do,' her godmother nodded, and Gina poured two cups of strong tea, adding milk and sugar to both. 'I'm worried about my son.' The subject was altered abruptly.

'Jarvis?' Gina spoke his name warily, but her mind had no difficulty in conjuring up a vision of a tall, dark-haired man with cold grey eyes and a mocking smile. 'He's a self-sufficient man with an established career as an attorney,' she added as she passed Evelyn her cup.

'He's also thirty-five, and I've lost count of the many women who had drifted in and out of his adult life,' her godmother explained with a measure of distaste. 'His latest is a hard-faced woman by the name of Lilian Ulrich, and the reason I am concerned is because his relationship with this woman has lasted much longer than any of the others.'

Gina did not particularly care for this discussion. Jarvis Cain, as a topic of conversation, had in recent years been shifted to the very bottom of her list of categories for discussion, but, for her godmother's sake, she pretended to show some interest.

'If he loves this woman, then surely——'

'Loves her!' Evelyn snorted in disgust as she stirred her tea with unnecessary vigour. 'He couldn't possibly love a woman like that! She's been married twice before, and her interest in men like Jarvis is purely for material gain. The only comforting thought I have to cling to is that marriage doesn't fit into my son's plans for his future.'

'You don't think Jarvis will ever get married?' asked Gina cautiously, and hating herself intensely for her curiosity.

'Not by choice, he wouldn't,' her godmother enlightened her, with a strange sadness replacing the displeasure in her grey eyes. 'And I'm afraid I am partially to blame for his cynical attitude towards marriage.'

Gina's sensitive features registered surprise.

'Why do you suppose that, Aunt Evelyn?'

'It's a long story,' Evelyn sighed, raising the gilded cup to her lips and taking a sip of tea. 'My husband and I made a mess of our marriage. We were both hot-tempered, stubborn, and too proud to admit our mistakes. Clement finally insisted on a separation, and I agreed . . . on condition that I would be allowed to remain here at Eldorado. I was hurt, and I retaliated by striking back where I knew it would hurt my husband most. It was, however, the cruellest thing I could ever have done, but at the time I didn't see it that way. Clement loved Eldorado with a passion which had been passed on to him by his father, and which Clement, in turn, has passed on to our son, Jarvis. It shattered my husband to leave his family home, and, God knows, I did eventually go to him in an attempt to set the matter right, but I failed. Clement chose to remain stubborn, and Jarvis consequently blames me for his father's early demise.'

'Have you explained this to Jarvis?'

'I have tried. Heaven knows, I've tried, but I'm afraid our cool and distant relationship doesn't exactly allow for the sharing of such intimate confidences.' Evelyn sighed again, but this time there were unmistakable tears in her eyes. 'Jarvis is a brilliant and sometimes ruthless attorney, and as a man he can be equally ruthless if he chooses. He has also inherited that hot-tempered, stubborn pride which drove his father and me apart. I am aware that my son has never forgiven me, and I often think that the only reason I still see him so frequently is that his love for Eldorado outweighs the resentment he harbours towards me.'

'Oh, surely not!' Gina could not believe that anyone could be so unforgiving towards this woman she loved so much. 'Uncle Clement has been dead for fifteen years or more!'

'I know my son, Gina,' Evelyn smiled, her mouth thinning with a touch of cynicism. 'Jarvis wouldn't turn a hair if I left every cent I possessed to charity, but Eldorado is quite a different matter. He wants this house, and I know he'll do almost anything to get it.'

A disturbing thought occurred to Gina. 'You're not thinking of depriving him of his home, are you?'

'Oh, no, my child,' Evelyn smiled again with that touch of cynicism which Gina found so disturbing. 'Jarvis will inherit Eldorado. Oh, yes, he will inherit it, have no doubt about *that*!'

There was something indescribably odd in her godmother's tone of voice, and for the first time in her life Gina felt uneasy beneath the intense scrutiny of those grey eyes. The clock on the mantlepiece chimed musically, alerting Gina to the fact that it was nine o'clock and long past the time when she should have left.

'Good heavens, look at the time!' she exclaimed, swallowing her last mouthful of tea. 'I'm leaving early in the morning for the farm, and I still have hordes of things to do before I go to bed tonight.'

'I shall look forward to Friday next week,' Evelyn smiled when Gina rose to kiss her wrinkled cheek. 'And give my regards to your family.'

Gina let herself out of the house. It was a dark February night, but that summer warmth was still lingering in the air as she slid behind the wheel of her blue Alfa and inserted the key in the ignition. She drove away from Eldorado, the twin beams of her car headlights slicing through the darkness down the circular drive. She left Houghton behind her and headed towards the centre of the city, but her mind was not focused entirely on what she was doing, or where she was going. Her conversation with Aunt Evelyn had left her feeling disturbed and decidedly anxious. She had known that her godmother suffered from angina, but she had never imagined that it could be this serious. It was a disquieting thought trying to imagine life without Aunt Evelyn. Ever since Gina's mother had died ten years ago, Evelyn had been there for Gina to talk to, to share her secrets with, and to weep on her shoulder occasionally about something that her father and her brother would not understand. Her death was something Gina did not want to think about, but it gnawed away at her until she arrived at her one-bedroomed flat in Hillbrow.

She packed a bag for the weekend, bathed, and got into bed. There was a stack of ironing to be done, but it would simply have to wait. If she wanted to leave early the following morning for her father's farm near Heidelberg, then she would have to have an early night.

But when she put out the light she could not fall asleep. She lay there in the darkness thinking about the conversation she had had with Aunt Evelyn, and the revealing information about her godmother's separation from her husband. *I'm aware that Jarvis has never forgiven me*—her godmother's remark leapt into her mind, and it left her wondering. Why had Aunt Evelyn chosen this particular evening to tell her about it? Why tell her at all?

Jarvis Cain. His strong features came unbidden on to the screen of her mind and she could not erase them. In recent years she had often seen his photograph in the daily newspapers, and always with a different woman clinging to his arm, but, as her godmother had pointed out, during the past months there had been only one woman—Lilian Ulrich!

Gina tried to shut her mind to these thoughts, but failed. Jarvis Cain had been nothing but a name to her until five years ago. His visits to the farm had never coincided with her school holidays, but on one particular Sunday, shortly after her sixteenth birthday, she had been sitting up in a tree, eating an apple, when her brother Clifford had shouted: 'Hey, George! Come down and meet Jarvis!'

She had looked down into smoke-grey, mocking eyes and, totally disconcerted, had lost her balance on the branch where she was perched. Jarvis had moved with a commendable agility. He had caught her smartly, his arms cushioning her fall, making her aware of the whipcord strength of his body, and Gina had fled the moment he set her free. Her embarrassment was something she had never forgotten, and neither had she forgotten his mocking laughter. It had followed her all the way to the stables where she had hidden until long after he left.

Whether by accident or design, she had seen him frequently after the incident. His charm, his brilliant mind, and his cynical attitude towards life made a fascinating combination to Gina at the age of sixteen, but, as a man of thirty, it was only natural that he had scarcely noticed her, and neither . . . thank God . . . had he noticed that she had developed an over-sized crush on him. For three years he had been her hero, the man of her dreams, but she had come to her senses at the age of nineteen realising that it was not worth her while bothering about a man who could pick up and discard women as easily as he did his clothing.

That was two years ago, and during this time she had avoided him as rigidly as she had tried to put him out of her mind, but she failed to do the latter on this occasion, and it was some time before she finally went to sleep.

The weekend at the farm might have helped Gina relax, but it did nothing to lessen her anxiety, and during the ensuing weeks she witnessed a deterioration in her godmother's health that filled her with a growing alarm. Evelyn never mentioned her health again, it was as if that discussion had never occurred between them, but her death, two months later, still came as a shock to Gina even though she had expected it.

It was her godmother's personal maid who telephoned Gina early the Wednesday morning to inform her that Evelyn had died quietly in her sleep. Gina had been almost too distraught afterwards to speak when she had telephoned home to give her family the news. The funeral was arranged for the Friday, and Gina took the afternoon off work to attend it. Clifford and his wife, Susan, could not come to Johannesburg for the funeral since Susan was expecting to go into hospital at any moment for the birth of their first child, but Gina's father arrived at her flat just before two that afternoon to accompany her.

Gina was pale but composed when she stood beside her father at the graveside. Facing them across the flower-decked coffin was Jarvis Cain, his tall, lean body clad in a dark grey suit which had been tailored to perfection to emphasise the width of his shoulders and the leanness of his hips. His tanned, perfectly chiselled features were set in those familiar lines of severity which had always filled her with awe, and the nervous leaping of her pulses was a startling indication that he still had the power to disturb her emotionally.

The shock of this discovery made her tremble, but she pulled herself together the next instant to hear the old priest saying: 'Forasmuch as it hath pleased Almighty God of his great mercy to take unto himself the soul of our dear sister here departed, we therefore commit her body to the ground; earth to earth, ashes to ashes, dust to dust; in sure and certain hope of the Resurrection to eternal life.'

Gina felt the steadying grip of her father's calloused hand beneath her elbow when she started to shake with suppressed tears, and when she finally raised her tear-filled glance it collided with Jarvis Cain's across the open grave. There was instant recognition in his steel-grey eyes, and there was something else that she could not define which disturbed her so much that she averted her eyes hastily.

Friends and family were beginning to disperse from around the graveside, and Gina and her father followed suit, but their departure was delayed by none other than Jarvis Cain.

'I'm glad you could come, Mr Osborne,' he said in his deep, well-modulated voice when he shook hands with Gina's father.

'We shall miss your mother,' Raymond Osborne replied, and Jarvis nodded gravely.

'So shall I.'

Did he mean that? Gina wondered. Or was he merely paying lip-service to a woman he had never forgiven for her unfortunate errors in the past?

'Hello, Georgina.' That deep voice interrupted her thoughts and, despite her height, she still had to crane her neck to look up into those cold eyes.

An unexpected shiver raced up her spine, and she lowered her gaze hastily to the hand he had extended towards her. She placed hers rather hesitantly in his, and felt a strange current of electricity passing through her that made her withdraw her fingers hastily a moment later.

'Hello, Jarvis,' she responded stiffly.

Had she imagined it, or had she seen a flash of mockery in his eyes in the second before he turned from her to speak to her father? She studied his strong profile, her glance taking in the broad, intelligent forehead, the straight, high-bridged nose, and the firm, jutting jaw. He had a beautiful mouth. His lips were sternly moulded with an exciting hint of sensuality in the curve of the lower lip, but at that moment there was a tightness about his mouth that heightened the severity of his appearance, and she wondered obscurely if he had forgotten how to laugh.

'I imagine you haven't had much time for leisure these past two years, but please feel free to come out to the farm for a weekend whenever you wish,' her father was saying, and Gina felt her body grow taut with nerves.

'Thank you very much for the invitation, and I shall take you up on it quite soon,' Jarvis promised.

He did not mean that. He was merely being polite. He would not really take her father up on his invitation, would he? Gina wondered frantically. Hell, she hoped not! She did not like the idea of Jarvis Cain visiting her home, and especially not when she was there. She had buried all her old feelings two years ago, and she did not want him to rake them up again.

Jarvis turned his dark head then and again their glances clashed. She saw him look at her rather oddly before he inclined his head briefly and walked away to talk to someone else, leaving Gina with the uncomfortable feeling that he had guessed she did not want him to visit her home.

Gina's niece was born on the Sunday afternoon, two days after Evelyn's funeral. Clifford had called Gina that evening to give her the news, and when she finally replaced the receiver she felt a mixture of excitement and melancholy surging through her. Evelyn's life had ended, but a new life had just begun, and Gina could not decide whether she should feel happy or sad.

During the course of that week she received a disturbing letter from Harold Ashton, Evelyn's lawyer,

asking her to call at his offices at her earliest conven-
ience. She made arrangements to see him the following
afternoon, and it was a shock rather than a pleasant
surprise to learn that Evelyn Cain had left her a legacy
of fifty thousand rand.

'There must be some mistake!' Gina protested, but
the stockily built man behind the cluttered desk shook
his head and smiled.

'There is no mistake, I assure you, Miss Osborne.
As soon as the estate is wound up I shall contact you
again, and if you need advice about investments I
shall be only too happy to assist you.'

Gina was in a complete daze when she went back
to work that afternoon, but the feeling of unreality
soon dispersed to leave her with an uneasiness she
could not shake off.

'You're not listening!' Mitzi Warner complained,
and Gina pulled herself together with an effort.

'I'm sorry,' she muttered apologetically, attempting
to focus her attention on her assistant. 'You were
saying?'

'It wasn't important.' Mitzi shook her blonde head.
'What *is* important is the fact that you went out this
afternoon and came back an hour later looking as if
you'd almost been run over by a bus. Did something
happen to upset you?'

'I've inherited a large sum of money from my
godmother.'

'Is that so terrible?' Mitzi demanded curiously, and
Gina took a moment to consider this.

Was it so terrible? No, not really, she answered
herself. It was simply that she felt so undeserving of
such a magnanimous gift, and she was also, curiously,
concerned about what Jarvis might think.

Gina went home to the farm at the end of that
week, and her pulse quickened on Friday afternoon
when she turned on to the Heidelberg road and left

the city behind her. It was always like this when she
went home, but this time there was the added excitement of seeing her little niece for the first time. Her
Alfa handled beautifully on the open road, and her
foot went down heavily on the accelerator when the
traffic lessened.

It was six-fifteen when she turned off on to the
gravel road that led to the farmhouse nestling among
the gum and poplar trees. The cattle were being herded
out of the grazing camp on to her right, and on her
left the *mealies* stood tall and green against the pink
haze of the sky at sunset. Ahead of her lay the big,
sprawling homestead with its wide, trellised verandah
along its front and east sides. It was an old house,
which had stood for several decades, and was home
to Gina.

Her father's dusty Ford truck stood alongside the
house, and Gina parked her Alfa next to it. She got
out quickly to breathe the country air deep into her
lungs, and she arched her tall, slender body as she
raised her face towards the setting sun. In brown
slacks and safari-type shirt she looked almost boyish,
but there was a natural feminine grace in the way she
moved when she took her bag out of the boot and
walked round to the front of the house. Her heart felt
lighter when she climbed the well-trodden steps up to
the verandah, and the outer door creaked with a
welcoming familiarity beneath her hand when she
entered the house. She left her bag next to the hat
stand and, following the smell of a roast in the oven
and freshly ground coffee, she crossed the carpeted
hall and walked down the passage into the kitchen.

A dark-haired woman, looking slender in a floral
summer frock after her months of pregnancy, turned
from her inspection of the dinner simmering on the
stove, and the corners of her bright blue eyes creased

into a welcoming smile when she saw Gina. 'You're just in time for dinner.'

'Hm . . . it smells good, Susan.' Gina kissed her sister-in-law's cheek and turned towards the grey-haired man who had risen from a chair beside the scrubbed wooden table. 'Hello, Dad.'

'We expected you half an hour ago,' Raymond Osborne announced accusingly when he had extricated himself from his daughter's fervent embrace, and he lowered his tall, lean body on to the chair he had vacated moments before.

'The traffic was rather heavy on the exit routes from the city,' Gina explained, turning eagerly back to Susan. 'Is there time to take a quick look at my niece before dinner?'

'Of course there is,' Susan laughed softly, wiping her hands on a cloth and leading the way out of the kitchen and along the passage to her bedroom where a tiny, pink bundle lay sleeping in a cradle. 'Isn't she beautiful?' Susan whispered proudly.

'Beautiful,' Gina agreed, smiling as she brushed the tips of her fingers lightly over the soft, dark hair. 'She looks like Clifford, but she has your dark hair, and if you're not careful I'm going to spoil her.'

'When are you going to find yourself a nice young man you can marry and have children with, Gina?'

Gina looked up sharply to meet her sister-in-law's steady gaze. 'I'm only twenty-one, Susan,' she protested.

'And I'm twenty-two with a husband and a child.'

'You were lucky enough to meet the right man,' Gina answered defensively, and with a certain amount of envy that she could not suppress.

'The trouble with you is you don't let any man get close enough to you, and if you don't do that you'll never find out if he's the right man for you.' Susan continued the argument in a lowered voice.

'That's not quite true,' Gina protested calmly. 'Norman Thorpe and I spend a lot of time in each other's company.'

'And how close do you let him get to you?'

'Close enough.'

'Within arm's length, mentally and physically, I presume,' grinned Susan, and Gina felt herself colouring in the dim bedside light.

'I don't want a physical relationship with Norman, and I don't feel the need to share all my private thoughts with him.' She turned away agitatedly until her face with in shadow. 'I don't want that kind of relationship with a man.'

'When the right man comes along you'll want to be physically close, and you'll want to share all your thoughts with him.' Susan spoke with quiet conviction.

There was only one man Gina had thought could make her feel like that, but he was beyond her reach. Anyway, she enjoyed her freedom, it was something she cherished, and she had no burning desire to change her lifestyle in a hurry.'

'I hope dinner is ready, because I'm starving.' Gina changed the subject, and Susan did not pursue the matter as she accompanied Gina out of the room.

Clifford had been out mending fences washed down by the recent rainstorms, but he arrived home in time to join them for dinner. His tall, bulky frame made the floorboards shudder beneath him when he entered the dining-room.

'Hello, George,' he smiled teasingly, his welcoming embrace almost a punishment. 'How's your love-life?'

Gina looked up at her fair-haired brother with stormy green eyes. 'Don't call me George, and mind your own business!'

'Cheeky as ever, I notice,' he laughed throatily, pushing a big, calloused hand through his unruly hair before he pulled out a chair and seated himself at the table. 'It's going to take a man of steel to keep you in order, little sister, and I don't envy him the task.'

He had inherited their mother's velvety-brown eyes, and they were laughing at Gina in a way that made an involuntary smile pluck at her generous mouth. 'I wonder sometimes why I tolerate you!'

He laughed again, a deep, thundering laugh, and it was so contagious that Gina laughed as well. Clifford was eight years older than Gina, and they were very close despite the fact that his teasing often drove her to anger. He was a warm, spontaneous and loving person. He was also fortunate to have found a wife like Susan who had fitted so perfectly into the family, and Gina could almost envy them their happiness.

It was late that evening before Gina got to bed, but she was up early the following morning and was not surprised to find her father and brother drinking coffee in the kitchen at that early hour.

'Why are you up this early?' her father demanded.

'I thought I'd take Jupiter out for some exercise,' she said, helping herself to a cup of coffee, and drinking it quickly.

'I'd be careful of that black devil, if I were you,' Raymond warned gravely. 'He's been stabled for two weeks without sufficient exercise, and he's been temperamental lately.'

'Gina should have settled for an even-tempered horse like Star,' Clifford intervened, turning to Gina with brotherly concern. 'You're going to break your neck on that horse one day if you're not careful.'

'Riding a horse like Star is like sitting astride a lifeless log, so I'll stick to Jupiter,' Gina laughed carelessly. 'See you both later.'

The sun had not yet risen when she strode out to the stables. Her father was right. The black Arab

stallion's magnificent body had not had sufficient
exercise, and he was extremely temperamental. Jupiter's ears flipped back when she approached his box,
a sure sign of bad temper, but Gina spoke to him in
a calm, soothing voice. He snorted, lifting his head
arrogantly, and pricked his ears as a signal that he
recognised her.

'Please bring me my saddle, Solomon,' Gina asked
the stablehand who had approached her, keeping her
voice lowered and calm for Jupiter's sake. Solomon
did so at once, even though his eyes widened with
alarm.

Gina rubbed Jupiter's black nose, and slid her hand
in a light caress along his neck while she continued to
speak quietly to him. She felt him quiver with
suppressed energy, and he stepped about restlessly,
eager for his freedom. She shot back the bolts on the
stable door when Solomon arrived, and he helped her
to saddle the spirited animal she had begged her father
to buy a year ago.

'He's a devil this morning, Miss Gina,' Solomon
warned when they were leading Jupiter out into the
yard.

'I can handle him,' Gina answered confidently, her
hands sliding along the quivering horse's neck, and
with no effort at all she was in the saddle.

Jupiter reared, his front legs clawing the air when
he felt her weight on his back, and Solomon leapt
back hastily with a jaundiced look on his face.

He shouted a warning, but Gina was not listening.
She was still firmly in the saddle despite the stallion's
efforts to dislodge her and, leaning forward, she
shouted close to his ear, 'Let's go, Jupiter!'

The stallion needed no further encouragement. He
sped across the yard and out through the open gate,
hooves thundering on the soft earth, and the wind

whipping through his mane as it whipped through Gina's red-gold hair. Sheep scattered in various directions when horse and rider raced across the veld, and pheasants fluttered noisily from their nests in the tall grass, but the cattle stood chewing their cud and seemed to view this wild escapade with such disdain that Gina's laughter rang out above the thudding of Jupiter's hooves.

She did not attempt to rein him in. She leaned forward in the saddle, her body moving in perfect unison with the rhythm of the horse, her hands on the reins acting simply as a gentle guide. The smell of the dew-wet earth mingled with that of horseflesh and creaking leather to add to the exhilaration of this exercise, and she revelled in her own freedom as much as Jupiter did in his.

Jupiter and Gina were in harmony with each other, and it was almost a joint decision to stop eventually on the crest of a hill to enjoy the silence and the beauty of nature at that early hour of the morning. Gina's gaze went beyond the neat rows of *mealies* to where the sun was rising behind the distant hills, and a predatory hawk had already begun to circle lazily in the sky, its keen eyes seeking a defenceless prey. Jupiter snorted, pawing the ground with renewed impatience, and Gina touched his sides lightly with her heels as an indication that she was ready to go.

The ride home was accomplished with less vigour but with equal enjoyment, and the early morning sun was climbing swiftly into the sky when they entered the yard at a slow trot.

A silver Jaguar was parked beside the house next to her Alfa, and a frown creased Gina's smooth brow. She knew no one who had a car like that, and a vague uneasiness stole through her when she reached the stables. She slid off Jupiter's back in a graceful, fluid movement, and gently patted the animal's neck, praising him absently in her soft, husky voice. Who on earth could be visiting them at this early hour of the morning? she wondered, as Jupiter responded to her praise with a whinny and a nudge against her shoulder before Solomon led him away.

The outer door slammed shut behind Gina when she entered the kitchen where Susan was supervising the breakfast preparations.

'We have a visitor,' Susan told her.

'So I've gathered.' Gina surveyed the activities in the kitchen with curiosity. 'Who is it?'

'Jarvis Cain.'

'Oh, lord!' groaned Gina, pushing her fingers through her windblown hair. She should have known! Something should have warned her that it would be Jarvis Cain!

CHAPTER TWO

GINA felt curiously faint as she stood staring at her sister-in-law. 'What the devil is Jarvis Cain doing here?'

'I understand he is here at your father's invitation, and I think he's quite devastatingly handsome.' Susan pretended to swoon, but her glance sharpened the next instant at Gina's taut features. 'Don't you like him?'

'Let's just say I don't *dislike* him.' Gina evaded Susan's query. 'When did he arrive?'

'About half an hour ago.' Susan scrutinised everything on the trolley before she turned back to Gina who stood hovering with indecision and uncertainty in the kitchen. 'Would you be an angel and tell the men that breakfast is about to be served in the dining-room?'

Nervous repugnance seemed to make Gina's insides coil into an uncomfortable knot. 'Do I have to?'

'There's no sense in hiding from him, is there, Gina?' Susan laughed but at that moment Gina could see no humour in the situation.

'I suppose you're right,' she agreed, attempting to hide her nervousness behind an outwardly casual appearance.

She walked out of the kitchen, and could feel her heart beating somewhere in the region of her throat when she followed the sound of male voices into the lounge. Jarvis rose from his chair when she entered the room, presenting an imposing figure despite the casualness of his cream slacks and sweater. His dark hair was brushed back severely from his broad forehead, and steel-grey eyes flicked over her in a swift, unflattering appraisal that made her embarrassingly aware of how she was dressed. Her riding boots were dusty, her blue denims old and faded at the knees and around her posterior, and there was a tear in the sleeve of her blue checked shirt which she had not bothered to mend when the collar had long since become frayed in the wash. She felt an annoying warmth steal into her cheeks, but there was a hint of defiance in her green eyes that withstood Jarvis's steady appraisal.

'Good morning, Georgina,' he acknowledged her politely, his deep, well-modulated voice sending a not unfamiliar tremor racing up her spine.

'Hello, Jarvis,' she responded with a calmness that did not betray the turmoil inside her, but her mouth felt curiously dry when she turned from him hastily to confront her father and brother. 'I was told to tell you that breakfast is about to be served in the dining-room.'

'Ah, come along, then, Jarvis,' her father smiled at their guest as he and Clifford rose from their armchairs.

Gina led the way across the carpeted hall into the dining-room, uncomfortably aware of Jarvis's eyes lingering on her body.

'You smell like a horse,' Clifford teased her tactlessly, heightening her embarrassment, and she turned on him with eyes that sparked green fire.

'How would you expect me to smell when I've just come in from a ride?' she demanded icily, and a look of surprise flashed across Clifford's rugged face. 'At any rate, I wasn't aware that we would have a distinguished visitor joining us for breakfast this morning,' she added acidly.

There was an awkward silence when they seated themselves around the dining-room table, and to her dismay, Gina found herself sitting directly opposite Jarvis.

'How many horses do you have on the farm?' Jarvis started the conversation flowing again, and his glance skidded away from Gina to Clifford.

'Six,' Clifford answered him, getting up to assist Susan with the laden trolley she was pushing into the dining-room. 'We have a gelding, four mares, and an Arab stallion which is exclusively Gina's.'

'Do you still ride, Jarvis?' asked Raymond, while Gina sat staring rigidly at the white tablecloth in front of her.

'Whenever I get the opportunity, and that's not often these days.'

'Gina takes Jupiter for a run early in the morning when she's home.' Clifford's statement made Gina stiffen with growing resentment. She knew what would follow, but she could not prevent it without a scene. 'Perhaps you would like to accompany her tomorrow?' Clifford confirmed her suspicions.

'I could think of nothing I would like more,' Jarvis replied smoothly, his compelling glance drawing Gina's across the table. Once again she had the disquieting suspicion that he was fully aware of the antagonism building up inside her despite her desperate attempt to mask her feelings. 'If Gina doesn't object to my company,' he added softly, his eyes challenging her.

Damn him! Jarvis was much too shrewd for her own comfort, and so confoundedly clever that she could almost hate him.

'I have no objections.'

Her faintly husky voice had been brittle with a suppressed anger which had not escaped him, and he smiled derisively.

'In that case, I accept the invitation gladly.'

Oh, doom! There was no way she could escape it now! She felt everyone looking at her as if they were aware of that odd tension in the air and blamed her for it, and it added to her discomfort.

'Bacon, Jarvis?' Susan stepped into the breach, her calm voice shattering the tense silence and easing the atmosphere.

'Thank you,' he smiled, passing his plate.

Gina made no attempt to contribute to the conversation during the remainder of that meal. She could not help thinking, however, that Jarvis looked out of place in his casual but immaculate attire while her father and Clifford were dressed in their usual khaki trousers and safari jackets, but it did not appear to cause Jarvis the slightest discomfort. He looked relaxed and completely at ease, while Gina sat rigidly on the edge of her chair as if she had swallowed a rod.

Clifford went out in the truck after breakfast to repair a broken fence on the northern boundary, and Jarvis accompanied him. Gina was greatly relieved and, except for having to face him again across the table during lunch and dinner that Saturday, it was Clifford and her father with whom Jarvis spent most of his time.

Gina was in the kitchen late that evening when she heard footsteps and voices disappearing in the direction of the bedrooms. 'Good!' she thought. 'Everyone's going to bed.' The tension eased out of her muscles, but the sound of footsteps approaching the kitchen made it return with an agonising force. She steeled herself for Jarvis's entry into the kitchen, but it did not prevent her nerves from reacting violenty at the sight of his tall, lean frame standing in the doorway.

His glance flicked over her, taking in the grey and green flecked tweed skirt and amber-coloured blouse which she had changed into after breakfast that morning.

'Does everyone always go to bed at this early hour?'

'That's farm life,' she shrugged with affected casualness. 'Early to bed and early to rise.'

'Makes a man healthy, wealthy and wise,' he completed the proverb with a cynical smile playing about his sensuous mouth. 'Why aren't you in bed yet, or has life in the city changed all that for you?'

She gestured towards the electric kettle which was on the boil. 'I like making myself a cup of coffee before I go.'

'May I join you for a cup of coffee?'

Oh, drat! Why couldn't he go to bed like everyone else and leave her alone?

'You're welcome,' she said abruptly, turning her back on him, but she could feel his cold eyes following every movement she made while she set out two cups and spooned instant coffee into them.

'You're so very polite, Georgina,' he mocked her as he pulled out a chair and seated himself at the kitchen table. 'I'm beginning to think that my presence here on the farm displeases you.'

Gina was not in the least surprised. She had suspected that Jarvis knew she did not want him there from the moment her father had issued the invitation at Evelyn Cain's graveside, and he was simply confirming her suspicions.

'You're my father's guest,' she answered him, hiding her discomfiture behind a calm and cool exterior.

'I'd like to be your guest too.'

Gina's hand shook unaccountably when she poured boiling water into the cups. There had been something strangely ominous about that remark, but she chose to ignore it.

'How do you like your coffee?'

'Black with no sugar, thanks.' She felt his speculative glance roaming over her when she turned to place their cups of coffee on the kitchen table, and he did not leave her waiting in suspense for his verdict.

'You've changed these past two years since you've been working and living in the city.'

'Have I?' she asked with a forced casualness as she seated herself at the table, but her heart was drumming uncomfortably hard against her ribs.

'It was five years ago that we met for the first time, and then you must have been . . . what?' His narrowed, questioning eyes were riveted to her face. 'Fifteen? Sixteen?'

'Sixteen.' She supplied the answer, stirring her coffee with unnecessary vigour in an attempt to shut out the memory of that first encounter, but Jarvis had no intention of allowing her to forget.

'I have a vivid recollection of a freckled-faced kid with a long red plait down her back,' he smiled faintly with his eyes intent upon her rigid features, 'and I must say you almost scared the hell out of me when you fell out of that tree.'

Gina hated him at that moment when she felt her cheeks flame. 'Do you have to remind me of that embarrassing incident?'

'I didn't get the impression that you were embarrassed, at the time,' he contradicted gravely. 'I got the feeling that I'd scared you rigid.'

'Wouldn't falling out of a tree have scared you?' She bit out the question.

'I'm talking about *before* you fell.'

'Nonsense!' she protested vehemently, his perception and memory astonishing her to the extent that she almost choked on a mouthful of coffee.

'You're still afraid of me, for some reason.'

'That's ridiculous!' she snapped defensively, but he was so accurate in his assumption that she did not dare look at him.

'I agree that it's ridiculous,' he mocked her, and she could feel his speculative glance sliding over her again.

'You've grown into a very beautiful young woman, Georgina.'

His voice was a deep, smooth velvet, and it seemed to brush against her nerve ends like an intimate caress that sent pleasurable tremors racing through her. She sensed an element of danger in Jarvis that made her want to run like a frightened animal, and she could only pray that she would not run directly into the trap he might be setting for her.

'Drink your coffee before it's cold.' She changed the subject, but Jarvis remained unperturbed.

'Tell me about yourself, Georgina,' he said, raising his cup to his lips and swallowing a mouthful of coffee. 'I have some time to catch up on, and I have a vague recollection that my mother mentioned something once about computers.'

'I'm a systems analyst at Becketts Engineering.'

'That sounds very impressive.'

Gina's body stiffened. 'I don't intend it to sound that way.'

'Don't be modest about your achievements,' he rebuked her quietly. 'What do you do when you're not analysing your computers?'

'I read and listen to music, or I go to the theatre.'

'Alone?'

She avoided his piercing, probing, grey eyes and shook her head. 'No, not alone.'

'I should have known,' his mouth twisted into a semblance of a smile. 'You're much too beautiful not to have the men hovering like bees around the honey jar.'

'There's only one man,' she protested without thinking.

'So it's as serious as that, is it?'

'I didn't say it was . . . ' She faltered, a flash of anger in her green eyes when she realised how skilfully he had wheedled this personal information out of her.

'Are you trying out your court-room tactics on me, Jarvis Cain?' she demanded icily.

'It's a great help in finding out the things I want to know.'

His bland admission was accompained by a mocking smile that sent her blood pressure soaring.

'I'm going to bed.'

'You can't go yet.' His hand shot out, gripping her wrist before she could rise from her chair. 'We're only just beginning to get to know each other again.'

She felt resentment building up inside her as she stared down at that strong, long-fingered hand with the fine dark hair on the back. 'I don't want——'

'And besides . . . ' he interrupted her sternly, 'you can't go to your room like the rest of the family and leave your guest sitting here alone, now can you?'

'Damn!' Gina breathed angrily. She felt cornered, trapped, and her own family had played a part in it.

Jarvis leaned towards her, his eyes narrowed and intent as he inspected her rigid features. 'Did you know that you still have a smattering of freckles on your nose?'

Her breath caught in her throat, and she jerked her hand free of his clasp. Was he trying to flirt with her? No! Men like Jarvis Cain did not flirt with women, they seduced them!

'If you want to take that early morning ride with me, then I suggest we both have an early night.' She changed the subject as well as the thoughts flitting through her mind.

'I think the lady wants to be rid of me,' he smiled twistedly.

'Yes, quite frankly, I do,' she confressed stiffly, pushing back her chair and rising from the table—on this occasion without being detained. Jarvis arched a sardonic eyebrow as he got up swiftly to bar her way with his tall, imposing frame.

'You're honest to the point of rudeness, aren't you?'

'If I have to be.'

'In that case I shall always know where I stand,' he mocked her as he pushed his chair under the table and stood aside. 'After you,' he gestured with a sweep of his hand.

Gina brushed past him, catching a whiff of his particular brand of masculine cologne, and it was wholly pleasing to the senses. *Dammit!* She did not want to find anything pleasing about Jarvis Cain.

He followed her out of the kitchen in silence, and when they paused outside their respective bedrooms, he glanced at her and smiled faintly. 'Goodnight, George.'

Gina drew a quick, angry breath, but he had gone into his room and she was staring at a closed door before a sound could pass her lips. How dared he call her *George*! Her hand was trembling with suppressed fury when she switched on her bedroom light and closed the door behind her.

She got undressed and went to bed, but it was a long time before she went to sleep. For some infuriating reason her mind had latched on to Jarvis, and she was recalling everything about him as if he was standing in front of her. The mere thought of his awesome presence made her body stiffen between the sheets, and she felt again his lean hand clasping her wrist. His grip had been firm, not painful, and she wondered if he had felt the quickening of her pulse beneath his fingers.

Oh, lord! Why did she have to lie there thinking about him? As a teenager she had had a crush on him which she had fought valiantly to overcome when she had realised the hopelessness of the situation. The circumstances had not altered over the years, but she was now an adult. She knew that her feelings, if aroused again, could become a great deal more complex, and that was what she was afraid of. The attraction was still there, and it would be foolish of her to ignore that it was stronger than before. If she did not place a guard on her heart she would fall in love with him all over again, but this time the consequences would be more painful.

Gina rolled over on to her side to bury her face in her pillow, and somehow managed to go to sleep.

There had been no need to set an alarm. Gina had always been an early riser, and she was awake long before dawn the following morning. She got up and dressed; in jodhpurs and a green, long-sleeved shirt that matched the colour of her eyes, she looked more respectable than the day before, and she was annoyed with herself when she realised that she had unintentionally dressed like this for Jarvis's benefit. Damn the man for affecting her in this way!

Gina left her room quietly and crossed the darkened passage to where a strip of light emerged from a door which stood slightly ajar.

'Jarvis, are you awake?' she asked unnecessarily.

'Come in,' he instructed.

She opened the door wider, and her breathing became oddly restricted. Jarvis was still minus a shirt, and she was staring at him as if she had never seen a naked male torso before. Her glance had become riveted to the wide shoulders, the bulging biceps, and the muscled chest with short, dark hair trailing down the centre to his taut, flat stomach and where his blue denims hugged his lean hips. She had never before encountered a man who could exude such an overpowering aura of raw masculinity, and her blood seemed to heated as it flowed faster through her veins.

'Good morning, Georgina,' he greeted her smoothly. He was in no apparent hurry to put on the black sweater he had taken out of the wardrobe.

His eyes glittered strangely when they met hers, and it took no more than a startled second for her to realise that he was very much aware of the effect he was having on her. Jarvis was, in fact, laughing at her, and she turned angrily on her heel, her cheeks flaming with embarrassment.

'I'll be down at the stables when you're ready,' she said coldly, and did not wait for him to reply before she walked down the passage and out of the house.

The stars were fading, and the first fingers of light were beginning to stretch across the dawn sky when Gina reached the stables where Solomon was saddling the two horses. Jupiter whinnied softly and stepped about impatiently when she approached him, and her soothing voice calmed him sufficiently while she checked the girth and stirrups. The sound of boots crunching on the loose gravel made her turn her head to see Jarvis walking towards her, but she averted her gaze almost at once to concentrate on what she was doing.

'Do you always get up at this unearthly hour?' he questioned her with that now familiar hint of mockery in his deep voice.

'It's the best time for a ride,' she answered him abruptly, her hands tightening on Jupiter's bridle when the stallion became agitated at Jarvis's approach.

'Which horse am I to ride?'

'That one,' she said, pointing towards the chestnut gelding with a white star on his forehead.

'Thank you.' He gave the black Arab a wide berth when it pawed the earth impatiently. 'Isn't that horse a bit too spirited for you?'

'Jupiter and I have an understanding.' She placed a calming hand on the horse's quivering neck. 'If I respect his freedom of spirit, he will tolerate my hands on the reins.'

'That sounds like animal psychology to me,' Jarvis mocked her, but Gina chose to ignore it as she watched him mount Star with the ease of a man accustomed to riding.

'Shall we go?' she asked.

'When you're ready,' he smiled faintly, and she had to admit to herself that he looked good in the saddle.

Gina mounted the temperamental stallion with a swift, fluid movement, and he reacted instantaneously to her, 'Let's go, Jupiter!'

Star was an admirable horse, but he was slower off the mark, and he did not possess Jupiter's lightning speed when they rode out across the veld. The thudering of their hooves shattered the early morning silence, and Gina made no attempt to curb Jupiter's wild charge. The wind whistled past her ears, blowing her Titian red hair away from the delicate features that mirrorèd her enjoyment, while her slender, supple body moved in perfect unison with the rhythm of the horse. Gina could almost forget about Jarvis, she could almost forget about everything as she sat astride that magnificent animal, but as they neared her favourite hill, Jarvis caught her up with an unexpected burst of speed which Gina had not expected him to coax out ot Star.

'Do you always ride at this wild pace?' he demanded, raising his voice above the sound of thundering hooves, and Gina smiled at him with a gleam of devilish mockery in her eyes.

'Isn't it invigorating?' she shouted back, and with very little encouragement Jupiter leapt ahead again, maintaining the lead until Gina reined him in on the crest of the hill.

She took her feet out of the stirrups and slid gracefully to the ground. She was tethering the horse to an acacia tree when Jarvis brought Star to a halt beside her.

'How kind of you to stop and give me a break,' he remarked with derision while he dismounted and tethered a snorting Star to the tree beside Jupiter.

Gina did not answer him. She walked a little distance across the damp earth, and was elated to discover that they were still in time to witness the sunrise.

'Look!' She pointed towards the east when Jarvis stood beside her, and his glance followed the direction of her pointing finger.

A golden hue was reaching higher and higher into the dawn sky, and several seconds later the sun appeared beyond the distant hills. The dew-wet earth sparkled and came alive as if an unseen, magical hand had touched it. Birds began to flutter noisily in the trees, and the familiar *kwaali* call of the pheasants floated up the hill towards them.

To watch the sun rise through the city smog isn't quite the same as this, is it?' Gina sighed contentedly, unaware that the rising sun was setting fire to her hair, and equally unaware that there was something more than casual interest in the eyes of the man who stood observing her intently.

'You're a child of nature, Georgina.' Jarvis's voice intruded on nature's symphony of the awakening veld. 'What are you doing in the city?'

She felt his eyes on her, but she could not look at him, and she pushed her trembling fingers into the pockets of her judphurs with a careless shrug of her shoulders. 'I have to earn a living somewhere, and if I can't do so here on the farm, then I shall have to do so in the city.'

'If you had a choice, what would you do?' His compelling glance drew hers and held it for a moment, and a tiny wave of shock charged along her nerve ends before she looked away.

'I don't have a choice, so your question is irrelevant, Mr Attorney,' she answered coldly, turning from him to walk towards the horses.

'I wonder where and how my mother got the idea that you were a sweet, gentle, and even-tempered girl,' he said, evoking in her a stab of longing for her godmother, and Gina halted abruptly in her stride to face Jarvis.

'Your mother was a wonderful woman, and I loved her very much.'

A cynical smile curved his mouth. 'My mother was also a woman who knew what she wanted, and she always made sure that she got it.

He sounded bitter. He also made Evelyn Cain sound like a conniving, manipulating old lady. Why? Was he so incapable of understanding and forgiving?

'I'm actually pleased that I have this opportunity to speak to you privately.' Gina determinedly broached the subject which had disturbed her since she had paid that visit to Aunt Evelyn's lawyer. 'I assume you must know about the money your mother left me in her will?'

His eyes narrowed in a way that sent a stab of fear through her, and he replied, 'Yes, I know about it.'

'I feel guilty about that inheritance because I don't consider that I ever did anything to deserve it.' She blurted out her feelings with her usual honesty.

'You meant a great deal to my mother, especially during these last few years,' he said with an odd tightness about his mouth. 'That was my mother's way of saying thank you, and I suggest you accept that inheritance without reservations.'

'If you say so,' she murmured, turning towards the horses, and feeling easier in herself now that she knew how Jarvis felt about the unexpected legacy from Aunt Evelyn. There was also something else she had to know, but she could not look at Jarvis when she asked, 'Did you talk to her before she died? I mean . . . '

'You mean . . . did I make my peace with her?'

'Yes,' she nodded, slanting a glance up at his tanned and unfathomable features with the short, dark hair lying in unruly, windblown strands across his broad forehead. 'Did you?'

That hint of bitterness was visible again in the tight smile that curved his sensuous mouth.

'We had a long discussion a few days before she died, and afterwards I thought we understood each other a gread deal better.'

He thought? Wasn't he sure? She observed him warily, and whispered an appropriate, 'I'm so glad.'

'So am I.'

They were standing barely a pace away from each other as the sun rose higher into the April sky flecked with stray clouds, and there was something about the way he looked at her that made her feel uneasy. It was time to return to the house, and Jupiter obviously thought so too. Gina was nudged between her shoulder-blades, the unexpectedness of it sending her stumbling into Jarvis. His hands shot out at once to steady her, but he did not set her aside immediately, and she was in the grip of a momentary paralysis when she came into contact with his hard, male body.

Her hands had reached out instinctively to clutch at his arms in an attempt to save herself, and she could feel the tautness of his muscles through the thin wool of his black sweater. Touching him like that sent an electrifying sensation rippling through her, and she tilted her head back, an apology hovering on her lips, but the words were stifled beneath his mouth.

Gina was too stunned at first to think of anything except the feel of that hard mouth so expertly drawing a response from her own. She tried to push herself away from him eventually, but one of his hands had found its way beneath her hair to the nape of her neck while the other had trailed down her spine to settle firmly in the hollow of her back, drawing her closer into the curve of his body until she could feel the unfamiliar hardness of male hips and thighs against her own. Her body went rigid with resentment at this suggestion of intimacy, but the next instant her pulse rate was escalating sharply. Jarvis's mouth was moving back and forth against her own with a sensual exper-tise that parted her lips for the invasion of his tongue, but a sweet stab of pleasure brought her abruptly to her senses. She thrust him from her with a burst of strength she had not known she possessed, and there was green fire in her eyes when she glared up at him.

'Damn you for doing that, Jarvis Cain!' She spat out the words, untethering the black Arab and leaping on his back. 'Come on, Jupiter, let's go home!'

Jupiter was in his element during that mad gallop down the hill and across the veld towards the house, and there was perfect co-ordination in that muscled body as Gina urged him on. She wanted to get away from Jarvis, and away from the sensations he had aroused with that kiss. As an adolescent she had often wondered what it would feel like to be kissed by Jarvis, but she had never dreamed that his kiss could awaken such stormy feelings within her. His mouth had been firm, warm, and pleasantly moist, and . . . God help her . . . she had actually enjoyed it! But how dared he! How dared he kiss her like that! And how dared he play with her feelings when he had a steady relationship with the blonde and beautiful Lilian Ulrich!

Gina reined Jupiter in as they approached the stables. He snorted loudly after the exhilarating exer-tion when she slid off his back and handed the reins over to Solomon. Jarvis arrived on Star seconds later, but Gina did not wait for him, walking on towards the house at a brisk pace.

'Georgina!'

She heard his quick, heavy footsteps behind her and felt his hand brush against her arm to detain her. She rounded on him with pent-up fury blazing in her eyes. 'Don't touch me!' she hissed.

'I shan't touch you if that's what you want, but it hadn't been my intention to offend you,' he said quietly, his hands raised in a gesture to appease her. 'The temptation to kiss you was quite irresistible, and I'll apologise if you really want me to.'

A gleam of mockery shone in his eyes together with a hint of challenge. He was much too clever for her, *damn him!* He was not a callow youth, and he must know how his kiss had affected her. To demand an apology would be ridiculous under the circumstances, and Jarvis knew that just as well as she did.

She drew a deep and calming breath as she forced herself to meet the challenging onslaught of his piercing glance.

'I guess I'm overreacting.'

'My dear, how charitable of you to say so.'

He was mocking her openly. She could hear it in his voice and see it in his eyes, and her temper rose again by several degrees, but she bit back a sharp retort as she turned from him to walk towards the house.

'Let's go and have breakfast.'

His deep-throated chuckle added to her annoyance when he fell into step beside her, but she looked straight ahead and desperately tried to ignore his lean, muscular presence next to her when they walked up the verandah steps and entered the house.

Gina made sure that she stayed out of Jarvis's way as much as possible during the course of that morning, but she could not avoid having to face him across the

luncheon table. She tried to ignore him, but at close
range or at a distance, she found that Jarvis was not
a man she could ignore. He had the personality and
bearing of a man accustomed to commanding everyone's attention, and Gina could feel herself slipping
back into the past when she had been fascinated
almost into a lovesick trance by his intelligence and
wit.

'No! Not again!' she rebuked herself sharply. She
would not fall into that trap a second time.!

Gina almost jumped for joy when Jarvis announced
that he was returning to Johannesburg after lunch,
and politeness forced her to hover in the background
when it was time for him to leave. There was a genuine
warmth in the exchange of words when he took his
leave of Raymond, Clifford and Susan. Gina, standing
a few paces behind the others when Jarvis got into his
silver Jaguar, was studying him speculatively when he
turned his head abruptly, and she was aware of that
familiar stab of shock when their eyes met.

His mouth twitched in a suggestion of a smile as if
he was aware of her reaction. 'I'll see you during the
week, Georgina.'

Not if I can help it! she thought angrily, and seconds
later the silver Jaguar was kicking up a cloud of dust
as it sped out of the yard and away from the farm.

A sigh of relief escaped Gina when they went inside.
Her family appeared intent on having a post mortem,
but she left them in the lounge to go to her room.

I'll see you during the week. Jarvis's parting words
echoed through her mind while she was preparing for
her own departure later that afternoon, and his remark
suddenly took on the proportions of a threat, but
Gina was determined that their paths would not cross
again unless it was absolutely necessary. She felt safe
away from Jarvis, and that was how she liked it.

CHAPTER THREE

THE Monday morning started badly for Gina. She had barely arrived at the office when she was enmeshed in problems that had arisen in the computer room. It was going to be one of those days when everything seemed to go inexplicably wrong, she could feel it, but Norman Thorpe telephoned her from his office before her spirits could sink too low, and invited her to dine with him the following evening.

'The Diggers restaurant is advertising a floorshow which I think you might enjoy,' he explained briefly, knowing her taste in entertainment, and she accepted without hesitation.

'I'll call for you at seven tomorrow evening,' Norman ended their brief conversation, and Gina left her office almost immediately for the computer room.

She did not return to her desk until two hours later, and she was gulping down a cold cup of tea when the telephone rang shrilly. Mitzi answered it and placed her hand over the mouthpiece before she turned to Gina.

'It's for you,' she said, 'and it's the second time this particular gentleman has called this morning.'

Gina frowned. 'Did he give his name?'

'No,' Mitzi shook her head, a sparkle in her grey eyes, 'but he's got the sexiest voice I've ever heard!'

Gina felt a stab of uneasiness when she lifted the receiver of the extension telephone on her desk. 'Gina Osborne speaking.'

'Good morning, Georgina.' Jarvis's deep, smooth voice came over the line when Mitzi replaced the receiver at her end. 'I trust you had a pleasant trip back to the city yesterday?'

Gina became aware of an unaccountable tightness at the pit of her stomach. 'I did, thank you.'

'Are you pleased to hear from me?'

No! she wanted to shout at him, but instead she injected a cool aloofness into her voice. 'Should I be?'

'Naturally,' he drawled, the mockery in his voice arousing her antagonism. 'It's twenty-one hours since the last time we saw each other.'

'I've survived.'

'You sound so cold and distant on the telephone, Georgina.' He was silent for a moment as if he were taking time to consider his own statement. 'What about having dinner with me this evening?'

'That's out of the question,' she declined his invitation abruptly.

'May I know why?'

Her mind was spinning in search of a reasonable excuse to offer him. 'I've got stacks of washing and ironing to do, and my carpets need a good vacuum.'

'Don't you have a serviced flat?'

'I'm not that fortunate.'

'What about tomorrow evening?' Jarvis persisted.

Thank God for Norman! Gina thought, when she could answer truthfully, 'I'm dining out with a friend.'

'Male?'

That hateful hint of mockery was still there in his voice, and she resented it. 'Does that surprise you?'

'Not at all,' he laughed shortly. 'You did mention that there was someone in particular, if I remember correctly.'

Gina was tiring of this conversation, and Mitzi was beginning to stare at her curiously. '*Look*, I'm very busy at the moment, and I don't——'

'Wednesday evening?' Jarvis interrupted her, and she had yet another valid excuse to offer.

'I shall be working late.'

'My, but you are a difficult young lady to pin down,' he laughed derisively. 'I shall simply have to try my luck some other time.'

Their conversation ended abruptly at that point, and Gina dropped the receiver back on its cradle as if she had been holding a poisonous reptile.

'Who was that, or shouldn't I ask?' Mitzi questioned her inquisitively.

'That,' Gina sighed heavily, 'was Jarvis Cain.'

Mitzi's eyes widened. 'Your godmother's son?'

'That's correct.'

'I gather he wanted you to go out with him, and you refused.'

'Yes, I refused,' Gina admitted, drawing a file towards her and pretending to study it while she took time to calm herself.

'Why?'

'Do you have to ask so many questions?' demanded Gina with a rare touch of irritation.

'Sorry.' Mitzi eyed her with a teasing, speculative look in her eyes. 'Isn't he as sexy-looking as his voice suggests?'

Gina sighed exasperatedly. 'If you must know . . . yes, he's *terribly* sexy, he's a knock-out, but I don't happen to be interested.'

'You're crazy!'

'Quite right,' nodded Gina, closing the file and pushing it across the desk, 'and if you haven't got anything better to do you can take this file through to the computer room.'

'Work, work, work!' Mitzi muttered reprovingly. 'That's all you ever think about.'

Gina leaned back in her chair with a jerky sigh the moment she was alone in the office. Jarvis's telephone call had left her disturbed and disorientated to degree she would not have believed possible. Her insides were shaking, and there was a tightness in her chest which did not leave her entirely for the rest of that day.

The Diggers restaurant was not a stylish place, but the food was good, and the floorshow consisted of a variety of entertainers doing their best to enhance the relaxing atmosphere. Gina needed to relax after having to endure two days of laborious activity at the office, and Norman was never a taxing companion. He demanded nothing of her except her friendship and her company, and that was the way she liked it. She was, nevertheless, exhausted when he left her at her door later that evening, and all she wanted to do was go to bed to sleep away the hours until morning.

Gina had known that she would have to work late on Wednesday evening, but she had not imagined she would be caught up in a mad race against time from the moment she stepped into her office that morning. The computer room staff began to snap under the strain, tempers were flaring, and Gina had difficulty controlling her own at times. She voluntarily cut her lunch-hour by half, and was in no mood for company when she stepped out of the building at one o'clock that day to see a silver Jaguar pulling up beside her. Paralysed into immobility at the sight of the man behind the wheel, she could only stare at Jarvis when he leaned across and opened the door on the passenger side.

'Lunch?' he invited, and raised a questioning eyebrow when she hesitated nervously. 'You do have time for lunch, don't you?' he prompted.

Gina stood as if she had become rooted to the sunlit concrete beneath her feet, but her heart missed several uncomfortable beats. 'I have half an hour.'

'Hop in,' Jarvis instructed curtly, and for some obscure reason she found herself obeying him. The interior of the Jaguar was luxurious, but she could not relax in the expensively cushioned seat when he steered the car into the stream of lunchtime traffic. 'I know a little place which is practically around the corner from here. There's ample parking, and the food is generally good.'

Gina did not answer him. She was too overwhelmingly aware of his lean masculinity in the dark grey, impeccably tailored suit, and the years seemed to roll back uncomfortably to fill her with that well-remembered feeling of awe which his presence had always aroused in her. As a young girl she had been aware mostly of his suave, handsome exterior, but as an adult she sensed in him a quality of steel and a ruthlessness which she imagined would make him a dangerous adversary in his professional as well as his personal life. Her rational mind told her that she had no reason to fear him, but there was something deep inside her that warned her of the threat he presented to her complacency.

Jarvis turned in a multi-storey car park, and drove up to the fourth level before he stopped his car and helped her out. Gina had no idea where he was taking her, but the lift swept them at a sickening pace up to the twenty-second floor of the building. The restaurant was new, the freshly painted sign indicating this, and the female patrons were elegantly dressed in the latest fashions. Gleaming silverware competed with glittering jewels, and Gina felt herself shrink mentally and physically from the scene confronting her.

'I'm not suitably dressed to enter a place like this,' she protested, and Jarvis paused in his stride to cast a critical glance at her pale green suit with the white silk blouse.

'You look perfect to me.' He offered his opinion after he had looked her up and down. 'Come, Georgina,' he instructed, taking a firm grip on her arm. 'I'm not in the mood for more excuses.'

His touch seemed to burn her skin through the cloth of her jacket when he steered her into the restaurant, and they were shown almost at once to a table for two. They ordered the salad speciality and coffee, and Gina glanced about her with interest while they waited. The walls were panelled and the lights were concealed in basket-shaped shades which hung low over the tables. It created a tranquil, intimate atmosphere, and she had no doubt that the cuisine would be expensive.

'Are you genuinely working late this evening, or was that merely an excuse not to dine with me?' Jarvis questioned her when their lunch had been served.

'I'm genuinely working late,' she confirmed, sampling her salad and attempting to relax despite the tight feeling inside her.

'Did you enjoy your dinner date last night?'

She looked up into mocking eyes and felt her back stiffen with resentment. 'I enjoyed it very much, thank you.'

'Did you spare a thought for me knowing that I would have to dine on my own?'

'I never thought of you once,' she lied, 'and I'm quite sure you would have had no difficulty in locating a female companion to dine with you if you'd tried.'

'You obviously think I'm in possession of a list of telephone numbers which I could plough through when in need of female company,' he smiled sardonically, and she lowered her gaze to the salad on her plate to hide her embarrassment at her own temerity.

'I never thought that at all, but I do happen to know that for some months now a certain woman has been featuring quite frequently in your personal life.'

'You are, of course, referring to Lilian Ulrich, but it's an unfortunate fact that Lilian is travelling around Europe at the moment.'

She felt him willing her to look at him, and her glance was drawn relentlessly to those cold grey eyes observing her intently across the table. 'I presume you are well aware that you're projecting an image of someone who is totally faithless and heartless?' she asked, staring at him with a mixture of annoyance and disbelief.

His eyebrows rose a fraction above his mocking eyes. 'I'm shattered to learn that you can think that of me.

'If you love her, then you ought to be faithful to her while she's away,' Gina rebuked him.

'Love her?' he laughed cynically. 'My dear girl, don't tell me you believe in all that romantic nonsense?'

She felt the coldness of shock spiral through her, but she pulled herself together almost at once. 'I'm not ashamed of what I believe in, and I can only pity you for being such a cynic.'

'You don't have to pity me for believing in something which can be explained and understood more accurately than love.' His voice was lowered and harsh. 'I'm talking about desire, in case you didn't know. When you want someone or something, you damn well know you do, and there's no doubt about it!'

Gina promptly lost her appetite, and she placed her knife and fork on her plate to drink her coffee instead. 'Desire is purely a physical thing,' she pointed out stiffly.

'Like sex?'

She almost choked on a mouthful of coffee, and glanced hastily at her watch. 'I must get back to the office.'

'Don't you like sex, Georgina?' Jarvis smiled at her mockingly over the rim of his coffee-cup, and she felt a wave of embarrassing heat surge into her cheeks.

'Do you mind if we change the subject?'

'I gather you had an inexperienced tutor who fumbled and ruined the whole thing for you.'

He was assuming that she was not a virgin, and she did not know how to correct him, or if, indeed, she even wanted to, but she found herself raising her hands to her flaming cheeks and wishing the floor would cave in beneath her. He was about to add something to his remark, but she forestalled him with an angry, 'Will you please stop it, Jarvis!'

His speculative glance sharpened, then he shrugged carelessly. 'The discussion has ended, if that's what you wish.'

Jarvis called for the bill, and Gina felt her colour subsiding slowly when they left the restaurant and stepped into the lift, but her insides continued to shake, and the little she had eaten seemed to lodge half-way between her stomach and her tight throat when the lift dropped down to the fourth level.

'Until what time do you expect to be working this evening?' Jarvis broke the silence between them when he drove out of the car park, and the sound of his smooth, unperturbed voice was infinitely annoying.

'Nine . . . or perhaps nine-thirty,' she answered briefly and evasively. 'I can't be sure.'

'Do you often work these late hours?'

'Not often.' His strong, long-fingered hands rested lightly on the steering wheel. He had nice hands. His fingernails were kept short and clean, and the warmth of his hand seemed to be lingering on her arm where he had touched her when they had walked to where he had parked the car. What was she thinking about! She gathered her scattered wits about her and made a concerted effort to concentrate on the topic of conversation. 'There's a mystifying error in the details which were originally fed into the computer, and as a result the computer is giving out incorrect data. The error has to be located and corrected, and we don't have much time in which to do it,' she explained.

Jarvis glanced at her briefly. 'Will you be working alone?'

'Some of the computer room staff will have to remain on duty,' she enlightened him when he pulled up in front of the grey building that housed the offices of Becketts Engineering, and her hand reached impatiently for the door-catch. 'Thanks for the lunch.'

Her mind was centred on flight, but Jarvis's hand gripped her arm to prevent her from leaving the close intimacy of his car. 'When do I see you again?'

'I don't know,' she gulped, wishing he would remove his hand from her arm if only to allow her to breathe easier.

'I'll give you a call,' he said abruptly, releasing her at last, but the familiar gleam of mockery was in his grey eyes as he added, 'and I can promise you, Georgina, I don't fumble when I make love to a woman.'

Her breath locked in her throat. If he had intended to shock her then he had succeeded. she also felt threatened, and her green eyes flashed at him in defensive anger before she got out of the car and slammed the door behind her.

Gina worked later that evening than she had anticipated, and it was long after ten o'clock when she arrived at her flat. She was tired, it had been a long, exhausting day, and her meeting with Jarvis had left her considerably disturbed.

She flung her handbag on her bed and kicked off her high-heeled shoes. The carpeted floor felt good beneath her stockinged feet, and she removed the combs from her red-gold hair, shaking the heavy strands loose until it bounced lustrously about her shoulders. What she needed now was a hot, relaxing bath before going to bed, but that hollow feeling at the pit of her stomach drove her into the kitchen to

make herself a cup of coffee. The doorbell rang before
the water could boil, and she switched off the kettle
with an exclamation of annoyance before leaving the
kitchen. Who could be calling on her at this late hour?

She opened the door as far as the safety chain
would allow, and her heart leapt nervously into her
throat. It was Jarvis, and his lean, hard body was
encased in snug-fitting black slacks and sweater giving
him a devilish and dangerous appearance.

'What are you doing here?' she demanded, her voice
so horribly husky and shaky that she barely recognised
it as her own.

'I have steak and chips from Antonio's around the
corner,' he announced, holding out a large package
for her inspection.

'You're crazy!'

'I'm hungry,' he corrected. 'Are you going to invite
me in, or do I stand here on your doorstep all night?'

Sheer astonishment made Gina hesitate before she
slid back the chain and opened the door to let him in.
He stepped inside and walked past her, casting an
appreciative glance about her cheaply but tastefully
furnished flat before he deposited the package of food
on the circlar table where she usually ate her meals.

'Jarvis, do you know what time it is?' she asked
dazedly, closing the door and walking across the room
to where he was taking the polystyrene containers out
of the brown paper packet.

'I'll get this ready while you fetch the knives and
forks,' was the only answer she received and, sighing
resignedly, she did as she was told. 'Ah, that's a good
girl,' he smiled briefly when she returned. 'Now sit
down and eat.'

Gina hovered beside the table, indecision gripping
her while he cut into his steak and sampled it with
relish. Her stomach twisted oddly and achingly,

reminding her that she had gone without breakfast that morning, and that she had barely touched her lunch at the expensive restaurant Jarvis had taken her to. Her mouth watered when she lowered herself on to her chair, the tempting aroma of the spicy steak too much to resist, and suddenly Jarvis's unexpected appearance did not seem so crazy after all.

'I didn't realise I was this hungry.' She broke the oddly companionable silence between them when she had swallowed the last morsel of food and leaned back in her chair with a satisfied sigh. Their eyes met, and Jarvis smiled at her in a way that made her heart do a crazy flip. For goodness sake, girl, she warned herself, don't go soft on a man like Jarvis Cain unless you want to be swallowed alive!

She gathered the empty containers together and got to her feet. When she felt her toes curling into the carpet she realised for the first time that she was still in her stockinged feet, but it was too late now to feel embarrassed about it. 'Coffee?' she offered.

'Yes, thank you, Gina.'

Her heart executed yet another flip in her breast as she turned towards the kitchen. That was the first time he had called her Gina, and she liked the sound of it on his lips.

She switched on the kettle for the second time that evening and made two cups of instant coffee, remembering that Jarvis drank his black without sugar.

Gina returned to the lounge to find that Jarvis had made himself comfortable on the sofa, and he gestured invitingly that she should join him there, but she chose to seat herself on the chair facing him. He observed her through narrowed, mocking eyes while they drank their coffee, and it unnerved her.

'Will you have dinner with me tomorrow evening?'

The invitation came without warning, but Gina was not going to allow herself to be startled into acceptance by his clever court-room tactics. 'Thanks for the invitation, but . . . no.'

A look of mild surprise flashed across his face as if he were not accustomed to women rejecting his invitations, but Gina had no qualms about it.

'Are you going to tell me why not?' Jarvis demanded with an element of danger in his quiet voice, and her body grew taut with the suspicion that she was being threatened.

'I have no desire to act as a stand-in for Lilian Ulrich.'

The knowledge that she might be encroaching on someone else's territory was only partly the truth. Jarvis was a man who would make demands on her which she could not and *would* not meet, and that was what frightened her.

'Did I say anything about wanting you to act as a stand-in?'

'No, but . . . ' Her empty cup rattled precariously in the saucer when her hands started to shake, and she put it down quickly on the small table beside her chair. 'Why this sudden interest in me, Jarvis?' she demanded with a bluntness which surprised even herself.

'My interest might have been aroused much sooner if you hadn't decided to go into hiding these past two years,' he mocked her, his narrowed eyes glittering strangely. 'You're an extremely attractive woman, and you shouldn't find it strange that I have a desire to get to know you better.'

There was a blatant sensuality in the smile that curved his mouth, and her breathing felt restricted when she rose to her feet to stand in front of the open window which overlooked the well-lit Hillbrow street with its ceaseless traffic. She did not hear Jarvis get up, she was too busy trying to control her pulse rate, but she felt him behind her, and she was aware of that power he exuded which seemed to enfold her like a restricting cloak from which there might be no escape.

'Now that we've met again I have no intention of allowing you to escape me, so you might as well tell that boyfriend of yours to shop around elsewhere,' he said as if to stress her thoughts, and the deep timbre of his voice was like a physical caress that sent an odd, tingling sensation surging through her body. 'You're going to be mine, Georgina, and I'm not going to let anyone or anything stand in my way.'

Fear and indignation ignited flames of anger in her green eyes as she spun round to face him. 'I shall never be yours, not even if you're the last man alive on this earth!' She spat out the words, but the only reaction she received was a smile that made her feel like a child whose behaviour was being observed with tolerant amusement.

'In the not-too-distant future I shall prove those words a lie,' he warned, his jaw set with a relentless determination that made her tremble inwardly. 'Goodnight, Georgina, and think about what I said.'

Gina stood frozen while he let himself out, and only when the door closed behind him did she come alive. She crossed the room quickly and slid the safety chain into position, but her hands were shaking so much that she had difficulty in accomplishing this otherwise simple task. She was scared out of her wits, and it took a concentrated effort to calm herself.

You're going to be mine, and I'm not going to let anyone or anything stand in my way. His words echoed repeatedly through her mind while she lay awake that night, and he had seemed so confident that it frightened her. What did he have planned for her? Did he want her as a mistress whom he could discard the moment someone else caught his eye, or did he want her as a wife? She ruled out marriage, and that left . . . ! No! She would rather die than become Jarvis Cain's mistress!

Gina did not sleep very well that night, and there were deep shadows beneath her eyes which her make-up refused to hide the following morning.

'You look as if you've had a bad night,' was the first thing Mitzi said when Gina walked into the office, and Gina did not attempt to deny it.

'I hardly slept at all,' she confessed tiredly, sagging into the swivel chair behind her desk.

'You take your work much too seriously, Gina.' Mitzi proffered her opinion, and Gina could not help wishing that overwork had been the only reason for the way she felt that morning.

She was fortunate that everything went off smoothly and without effort during her first few hours in the office, but the day started going awry at eleven when the telephone rang shrilly.

'It's for you, Gina,' Mitzi said a second later with her hand over the mouthpiece. 'It's the man with the sexy voice.'

Gina's palms felt damp. 'Tell him I'm not in the office.'

'I'm sorry, sir, but she's not in the office at the moment.' Mitzi obeyed Gina, but her glance darted nervously in her direction a second later. 'Just a moment, sir.' She placed her hand over the mouthpiece again. 'He says he knows I'm lying. What do I do now, Gina?'

'I'll take it,' Gina sighed resignedly and, steeling herself, she lifted the receiver on her desk. 'Hello, Jarvis.'

'Shame on you, Georgina, for encouraging that young lady to lie to me,' he rebuked her mockingly, and the velvety smoothness of his voice sent little shivers racing up her spine which were not altogether unpleasant.

'What do you want?' she demanded abruptly.

'Did you spare a thought for what I said last night?'

'No, I did not!' she snapped indignantly.

'Then I suggest you do, Gina, because I was deadly serious,' he warned in a way that made her feel choked with fear and something else which she refused to analyse.

'Go to hell, Jarvis!'

She slammed down the receiver, breathing heavily as if from an unaccustomed exertion.

'Well, that was brief and rather heated, wasn't it?' Mitzi remarked teasingly, and Gina's stinging reply was interrupted by the ringing of the telephone on Mitzi's desk. Mitzi answered it, and her glance shifted at once to Gina. 'Just a moment,' she told the caller before placing her hand over the mouthpiece. 'It's *him* again.'

Gina felt her insides starting to quake. 'Tell him I don't want to speak to him.'

'She said to tell you she doesn't wish to speak to you,' Mitzi informed Jarvis, but seconds later her eyes widened in something close to alarm. '*Yes,* sir . . . *certainly,* sir.' Gina would not dare hazard a guess at what Jarvis had said to Mitzi, but her assistant looked shaken when she replaced the receiver, and she did not keep Gina in suspense. 'He said to tell you that he wants you to have dinner with him this evening, and since you don't wish to speak to him, he'll take your silence as acceptance.'

'Like *hell* I'll have dinner with him!' exploded Gina, reaching for the telephone book to look up Jarvis's number at his office.

'He also said he'd pick you up at seven this evening, and you were not to keep him waiting,' Mitzi added breathlessly.

'Oh, how I'd love to give that man a piece of my mind!' Gina muttered as she punched out the number

on the telephone. A brisk female voice answered, and
Gina said abruptly, 'Mr Cain, please.'

'I'm sorry, but Mr Cain has just this minute left the
office, and he'll be in court for the rest of the day,'
the woman informed Gina. 'Could I perhaps be of
assistance?'

Gina felt deflated. 'No . . . it doesn't matter . . .
thank you.'

'Did he refuse to speak to you?' Mitzi wanted to
know, and Gina shook her head as she replaced the
receiver.

'He's left the office, and he won't be in for the rest
of the day.'

Mitzi nibbled thoughtfully at her cherry-red lip. 'If
there's no way to contact him, then I guess you'll
simply have to have dinner with him this evening.'

Gina was not in the mood to admit defeat. 'I don't
have to do anything I don't want to do.'

'In that case, I'm glad I shan't be in your shoes
when he arrives at your flat this evening,' Mitzi
announced firmly.

Jarvis arrived at her flat at precisely seven o'clock that
evening. At any other time Gina might have been in
a high state of nerves, but not on this occasion. She
was furious, her anger had been simmering all day,
and her eyes glittered with green fire when she
confronted him. A hidden and treacherous part of her
registered that he looked magnificent in an evening
suit, but she was momentarily blind to his masculine
appeal.

'You're not ready,' he accused, his sweeping glance
taking in her comfortable slacks, shirt and low-heeled
sandals.

'And *you* had no right to take it for granted that I
would agree to have dinner with you this evening,'
she counter-accused, her eyes blazing up into his with

a fury that was about to erupt. If she had not been so
angry she might have noticed the warning signals in
the tightening of his jaw and the icy glitter in his grey
eyes, but she was totally unprepared for what followed.
Steely fingers latched painfully on to her arm, and she
was marched unceremoniously across the lounge and
into her bedroom. 'What do you think you're doing?
Let go of me!'

'Shut up!' Jarvis instructed harshly, releasing her
arm to wrench open the doors of the built-in cupboard,
and she stared at him in something close to horror.

'How dare you open my cupboard and search
through my clothes?' she demanded, her fury rising to
a new level.

He hauled out a silky, ivory-coloured evening dress,
studied it for a moment, and flung it across the foot
of her bed. 'Put that on!'

'You can't make me!' she almost shouted at him,
realising at last what this was leading up to, and his
cold eyes narrowed to dangerous slits.

'Don't challenge me, Georgina, because I shan't
spare your blushes if I have to dress you personally.'
He towered over her, his manner adding conviction to
the threat in his voice, and something in her expression
must have conveyed to him the knowledge that he
had won. A semblance of a smile twisted his mouth
as he glanced at the gold watch strapped to his strong
wrist. 'You've got ten minutes, so make it snappy!'

He turned on his heel and, removing the key to
prevent her from locking herself in, he closed the door
firmly behind him. Gina felt trapped, beaten, but the
fight had not gone out of her yet. He had won this
round, but she was determined that the next round
would be hers.

She picked up the dress which Jarvis had flung
across her bed, and recognition made her eyes widen
in alarm. She had been in a crazy mood when she had

bought it the previous summer, but she had never summoned up sufficient courage to wear it. She did not want to wear it now, but, taking Jarvis's present mood into consideration, she did not think it wise to emerge wearing anything other than the dress he had selected.

She studied herself in the mirror a few minutes later, and wished she could hide rather than walk out of that room to confront Jarvis. The silky folds of the material were held together on her shoulders with pearl-studded slips to leave her arms as well as a considerable amount of the rest of her anatomy bare. It dipped low in front, too low for comfort, and the back plunged down almost to her waist. The dress fitted snugly about her narrow waist, and her hands trembled when she nervously fingered the skirt which flared out in soft pleats from her hips. She was adding a touch of coral-pink to her lips when the bedroom door was opened abruptly, and her heart lurched wildly in her breast.

'Are you ready?' demanded Jarvis.

Gina took a deep, steadying breath before she turned and said coldly, 'It's customary to knock before you enter someone else's bedroom.'

Her reproving remark made not the slightest impression on Jarvis, and it was Gina who finally stood cringing inwardly beneath his gaze. He devoured her slowly with eyes in which hidden fires had been lit, and his glance lingered deliberately on the shadowy cleft between the soft swell of her breasts. She had the oddest sensation that he was mentally stripping away the silky material to touch her with his eyes, and her body responded in a way that heightened her alarm. Her breasts grew taut, the nipples thrusting against the soft, restraining material, and a fiery warmth surged into her cheeks when a slow, sensuous smile curved his mouth. Jarvis was not a fool, and neither

was he blind. He was aware of the way she was
reacting, and there was a ring of triumph in his soft,
throaty laughter which made her hate him at that
moment.

'You should wear something like this more often,'
he said, his warm glance trailing over her once again
with the same shattering results. 'You have a beautiful
body, and you should be proud of it, but for some
obscure reason you always take great care in hiding
it.'

'When I want your opinion I'll ask for it and pay
for it like everyone else,' she retorted icily, picking up
her wrap and draping it about her shoulders as if it
were a shield.

'My opinion I give freely, Georgina,' he answered
smoothly. 'It's my advice I charge for.'

Gina flashed him an angry glance which was lost
on him as he ushered her out of her flat and down to
where he had parked his Jaguar. A wave of helplessness threatened to engulf her, but she would not
surrender to it, and she maintained a stony silence in
the car during the drive to the restaurant.

CHAPTER FOUR

THE restaurants Gina had frequented in the past seemed shoddy in comparison with the elegance and extravagance of the décor at Vittorio's. Candlelit tables in pillared alcoves offered the diners seclusion and privacy, and part of the floor was clear for dancing to the music provided by the four-piece band on a dais in one corner of the restaurant. Vittorio himself welcomed them at the door, and the lean, dark-haired Italian bowed low over Gina's hand when Jarvis introduced them.

'I have your usual table prepared for you, Signor Cain,' Vittorio announced, leading the way, and their footsteps were muted on the thick pile of the wine-red carpet. 'What about a good bottle of wine while you study the menu?' the Italian suggested when they were seated.

'I'll leave the choice and vintage to you, Vittorio,' Jarvis agreed pleasantly.

'I have a very special Italian wine in the cellar, and this is a very special occasion, is it not?'

Gina was aware of the flattering appraisal of those dark Latin eyes when she had summoned up sufficient courage to remove her wrap and drape it across the back of her chair.

'It is a very special occasion,' Jarvis agreed, his eyes glittering with laughter in the candlelight.

Damn the man! He seemed to read her like a book, and it was disquieting to know that she could not hide her discomfiture from him.

'I will have the wine brought to your table at once,' Vittorio told Jarvis, and then they were alone.

The music was rhythmic and soothing, but Gina was incapable of relaxing while she made a pretence of studying the menu. Several couples had ventured on to the dance floor to sway in time to the foot-tapping beat, but her feet felt like lead beneath the table.

The wine waiter brought a bottle to their table. Jarvis nodded his approval after he had tasted it, and their glasses were filled with the rich red wine which had been cultivated in the vineyards of southern Italy. Gina took a sip to steady herself, and found it smooth and fragrant.

Vittorio came to enquire whether the wine was to their liking, and that flicker of curiosity in his eyes before he walked away made Gina glance at Jarvis with a faintly derisive smile curving her soft mouth. 'Vittorio must surely be more accustomed to seeing you here with Lilian Ulrich,' she remarked.

'Forget about Lilian!' Jarvis instructed, his jaw hardening. 'Tonight it's you and me, Gina, and I won't have anyone else intruding!'

'You shouldn't cast people aside like old garments the moment they're of no further use to you.'

'And you shouldn't look so beautiful when you're indignant and angry,' he countered, placing her at a disadvantage. 'What would you like to eat?'

Gina stared with unseeing eyes at the menu in her hands, and closed it decisively. 'I'm not very hungry.'

'If you're determined to be obstinate, Georgina, then I shall have to order for you.'

Jarvis, she discovered, was not a man to make idle threats, and he demonstrated this by beckoning the waiter and proceeding to order without consulting her again. Her resentment finally gave way to fear, and she knew she would have to tread carefully in future.

'Relax, my dear.' He smiled at her across the table when the waiter had left, and his glance lingered with a hint of insolence where the parting folds of her evening gown allowed him a tantalising glimpse of the curve of her breasts. 'You look delectable, but I'm not going to eat you.'

Gina felt a wave of heat surge into her cheeks, but her glance did not waver. 'Your charm is wasted on me, Jarvis,' she said coldly.

'You're playing hard to get, and I must warn you that I thrive on a chase.' His sensuous mouth curved with mockery, but his grey eyes glittered like chips of steel when he rose to his feet and held out his hand to her. 'Shall we dance?'

It was an invitation, but she had the strangest feeling it was primarily a command, and she was annoyed when she found herself obeying. Her hand was in his as he led her on to the floor, and Gina had dreaded this moment, but she could not avoid it. His arm went about her, his hand touching her bare back, and her body stiffened at the electrifying sensations that spiralled through her. Being this close to Jarvis seemed to throw the natural mechanism of her body into discord, and her steps faltered.

'For God's sake, relax, Gina!' he growled close to her ear, and she had to make a determined effort to do as she was told.

She focused her attention on the music, and tried to forget that it was Jarvis with whom she was dancing. The latter was quite impossible, but her steps matched his beneath his expert guidance, and her tension waned as her enjoyment increased. His arm tightened about her, bringing her body closer to his until his thighs brushed against hers, but she had lost the desire to object as a strange warmth erupted deep inside her to spread throughout her body, and with it came the unquestionable knowledge that this was where she had always known she belonged.

> Such a feelin's comin' over me,
> there is wonder in 'most everything I see . . ..

A member of the band had started to sing the Richard Carpenter composition *'Top of the World,'* and those opening bars were so appropriate that a sigh parted her soft lips. Jarvis smiled down into her eyes in a way that made her heart miss a beat. Had he guessed her feelings?

The music ended soon afterwards, and Gina drifted slowly down from that blissful cloud when Jarvis led her back to their table with his arm still lingering about her waist.

'That wasn't so bad, was it?' he questioned her when they were seated facing each other across the table, and she shook her head.

'You dance very well.'

'I've had experience.'

There was a sensuality in his voice that gave a deeper meaning to his remark, and the corners of her mouth lifted in an involuntary smile. 'Yes, I'll bet you have!'

'Gina, I detect a naughty look in your eyes,' he teased, his glance meeting hers over the rim of his wine glass. 'Could it be that you're referring to sex, and not dancing?'

Her eyes sparkled with humour as she raised her glass to her lips, but she was not going to be provoked into answering that question.

'Have you moved into Eldorado?' She changed the subject.

'Not yet.' He smiled faintly as if he had probed her thoughts. 'For the moment I still prefer my flat in town.'

'Eldorado is not a house that should stand empty,' she voiced her opinion. 'It needs to be lived in.'

'It won't be standing empty,' he assured her with an odd smile curving his mouth. 'Not for long, anyway.'

The arrival of the waiter interrupted their conversation. Jarvis had ordered a seafood dish for himself, but for Gina he had chosen a small fillet steak with a spicy sauce, tiny potatoes, and a salad. Gina's appetite had been non-existent after their arrival at the restaurant, but suddenly she was ravenously hungry.

'It's been a pleasant evening so far.' Jarvis raised his glass when they were alone. 'Let's drink to the rest of it.'

Gina found herself agreeing with him. It had been pleasant, so why not drink to the rest of it? she thought, touching her glass to his before she raised it to her lips.

The dinner was superb, and when they had been served with a cup of aromatic coffee, Gina leaned back in her chair with a sense of well-being. It was at this point that she began to feel the after-effects of her sleepless night. Her body felt lethargic, and twice she had to stifle a yawn on the pretext of dabbing her lips with her table napkin.

They talked while they drank their coffee, and it was much later when Jarvis drew her again on to the dance floor. He held her close while they moved in time to the throbbing rhythm of the music, and Gina's blood began to pound through her veins with a rhythm of its own when his fingers trailed a path along the hollow of her spine. The sensations his touch aroused were wholly pleasurable and, coupled with tiredness, robbed her of the desire to resist. She relaxed against his hard body and her head went down on to his shoulder as if that was the most natural place for it to be.

Gina was drifting in a heaven of her own making, but when her steps faltered, he held her a little away from him and looked down into her sleepy eyes. 'I think it's time I took you home.'

'Yes, I am rather tired,' she admitted with a self-conscious laugh when he led her off the floor.

Jarvis placed her wrap about her shoulders, and his hands lingered there for a moment with a strange possessiveness before he escorted her out of the restaurant. The plush, comfortable interior of the Jaguar and the soft hum of its engine seemed to enfold her, and she was almost asleep when Jarvis pulled up at the well-lit entrance to the yellow-brick building in Hillbrow.

'Are you going out to the farm this weekend?' he questioned her in the lift which swept them up to the sixth floor.

'Yes, I am,' she answered him, wondering at the reason for his query.

'Then I dare say I shan't see you until Monday week.' He answered her unspoken query as the lift came to a halt and the doors slid open. They walked the short distance to her flat, and Jarvis took the key from her to unlock the door. 'Will you let me see you again?' he asked, following her inside.

Her mind warned against it. She was ill-equipped to cope with a man like Jarvis, and she was vulnerable. But somehow she heard herself saying, 'If you really want to.'

'I want to,' he smiled, faintly trailing his fingers along the curve of her cheek to her firm, rounded chin.

'Are you staying for a cup of coffee?'

What was she saying? It was late and she was exhausted, but for some obscure reason she did not want him to go.

'I'd like to accept your invitation, but you're wilting on your feet.' He smiled and touched his lips to hers in a warm, fleeting caress that quickened her pulse rate. 'Goodnight, Gina.'

'Jarvis . . . ' Her voice was a husky whisper and he turned with his hand on the doorknob to observe her curiously. 'Thanks for a lovely evening,' she finished lamely.

An unfathomable expression flitted across his lean, deeply tanned face, and she was wondering what he must think of her when she found herself crushed against his hard body. Her head went back, her red-gold hair spilling across the dark sleeve of his dinner jacket, and her soft, pink lips parted in an unconscious invitation he did not ignore. His mouth swooped down on hers, taking what she had so unintentionally offered, and Gina was plunged into a crazy world of clamouring emotions she had not known she possessed. Her wrap and handbag had slid to the floor, and his fingers were trailing in a sensual caress along the sensitive hollow of her spine. She trembled and clung unashamedly to his shoulders while she lost herself in the sensations his touch was arousing. And then she was set aside firmly.

'Sweet dreams, George,' he smiled twistedly, brushing his knuckles lightly against her flushed cheek. Then he was gone, leaving her confused and bewildered by the stormy response he had awakened in her.

Her hands were shaking when she slid the safety chain into position, and she cursed softly when she bent down to pick up the wrap and handbag. What was happening to her, and why did she invite him to kiss her like that? She had a feeling that she knew the answer, but for some inexplicable reason she was afraid to probe too deeply.

It was during the course of the following morning that an enormous arrangement of pale pink roses was delivered to her office.

'This can't be for me!' Gina protested when it was placed on her desk.

'It most certainly is,' laughed Mitzi, detaching the small white envelope from the decorative white ribbon and passing it to Gina. 'Aren't you going to open it?' she prompted almost impatiently when Gina hesitated.

Gina nodded speechlessly, and lifted the flap to extract the small card. Her heart was thudding against her ribs when she stared at the words written in bold black letters, and she could almost feel the steely strength of the hand that had penned them.

Until Monday. JC.

'What does it say?' demanded Mitzi.

'You're much too inquisitive,' Gina admonished her with a teasing smile hovering about her mouth.

'They're from Jarvis Cain, aren't they?'

'Yes,' Gina admitted, and Mitzi pressed her hands to her breast while her eyes rolled towards the ceiling in a swooning attitude.

'Oh, how romantic!'

Gina could not curb her laughter. It bubbled past her lips and, dropping the card into her desk drawer, she got up to place the arrangement on the cabinet against the wall. The delicate fragrance of late autumn roses filled her nostrils, and she gently fingered the satiny petals. She had somehow never imagined Jarvis to be the type to send a woman flowers, but then there was so little she really knew about him.

Norman walked into their office later that morning, and his eyebrows rose in surprise when he noticed the roses. 'Do you have a secret admirer?' he enquired.

'I . . . not exactly.' Gina was annoyed with herself. Why on earth should she feel guilty? 'They're from Jarvis Cain.'

Her confession seemed to convey something to him, and an odd expression flitted across his face as he dropped a file on her desk and left the office without a word. Gina stared after him, not quite sure how she was to interpret his behaviour, but the ringing of the telephone interrupted her thoughts, and she brushed the matter aside.

Gina went home that weekend with the hope that she would be able to escape from the events of the past week, but she could not rid her mind of Jarvis. He seemed to haunt her like a ghost wherever she went until she was aware only of an increasing desire to be with him, and to talk to him. It angered her that she could feel like this, but she was incapable of doing anything about it.

Until Monday, Jarvis had written on that card accompanying the roses, and excitement mingled with impatience when she returned to Johannesburg on Sunday afternoon. 'This is ridiculous!' she tried to tell herself, but the feeling persisted and grew until her longing for him was like an ache deep inside her. She recognised the signs—she was on the verge of falling in love with him all over again, and her heart would not listen to logic.

Gina had left the farm rather late, and it was after six that evening when she arrived at her flat. She unpacked her suitcase, bathed and washed her hair, and changed into a long-sleeved floral dressing-gown that zipped up the front. She used the hand drier on her hair and brushed it vigorously before she went into the kitchen to make herself some coffee, but she had not completed that task when her doorbell rang.

'Jarvis!' she gasped moments later, her treacherous heart missing a suffocating beat before it went on the rampage, and she stared at his tall, imposing frame as if he were an apparition her mind had conjured up. 'Just a moment,' she said, pulling herself together.

She closed the door, slid back the safety chain, and opened the door again to let him in. The now familiar scent of his cologne stirred her senses when he stepped inside, and she closed the door hastily to shut out the cold April breeze that had wafted in with him.

'I couldn't wait until tomorrow,' he explained, 'so I took a chance that you would invite me in for that cup of coffee I turned down the other night.'

Clad in beige slacks and polo-necked sweater beneath a brown leather jacket, he exuded a masculinity that threatened to take her breath away, and she turned away from the mocking scrutiny of those steel-grey eyes in the hope that her heart would ease its wild pace. 'I was in the process of making myself a cup of coffee,' she told him.

'Then I timed it perfectly,' he said, and to her dismay followed her into the small kitchen, his presence somehow dominating the limited space. She switched on the kettle and took down a second mug to spoon instant coffee into it, but she was aware of Jarvis with every fibre of her being, and she prayed that he would not see the tremor in her hands. 'Did you miss me?' he added.

His unexpected query almost startled her into revealing the truth, but she controlled herself in time. 'Was I supposed to?'

'Don't be evasive when all I require is a straight yes or no!' His voice was harsh, and his hand on her shoulder spun her round until she was looking a long way up into his equally harsh face.

'I feel as if I've been put into the witness stand!' She laughed to ease the tension that had risen between them, and she altered her voice dramatically when she added: 'Please answer the questions put to you, and remember you are on oath!'

'Well?' he demanded.

'I did find myself thinking about you at odd times,' she confessed when the look in his eyes warned her that nothing but the truth would suffice.

'Ah!' he sighed, a flicker of triumph in his razor-sharp eyes.

'Does that tell you what you want to know?' she asked with a hint of mockery in the smile that curved her sensitive mouth.

'No further questions.'

'I don't believe it!' she exclaimed in mock surprise, turning from him when the kettle boiled, and moments later she faced him again with a mug in her hand. 'Your coffee, Mr Attorney.'

'Thank you, George.'

Their fingers touched briefly as the mug exchanged hands, and a current of electricity seemed to shoot up her arm. 'Don't call me George!'

'Don't call me Mr Attorney,' he countered mockingly.

'Do we have an agreement on that?' Their glances met and held, making her realise that their present conversation was merely a cover for that almost static mutual awareness.

'We have.' He inclined his head slightly.

'Wonderful!' Her voice was flippant, but her pulses were racing, and it took a concentrated effort to break free of the spell she was certain he was casting on her. 'Shall we drink our coffee in the lounge?'

Jarvis did not react at once, and her heart leapt. His glance lingered briefly on the pulse beating frantically at the base of her throat before he stepped aside and allowed her to pass. If Gina had imagined he would give her a little more room to breathe in the lounge, then she was mistaken. His fingers snaked about her wrist, and she was forced to sit next to him on the sofa. Her alarm spiralled, but somehow she succeeded in looking outwardly calm.

He shrugged himself out of his leather jacket, and the muscles rippled beneath the expensive sweater which was moulded to his powerful chest and arms.

He questioned her about her family while they drank their coffee, and their mundane conversation somehow eased the tension from her body until she began to relax her guard. That was what Jarvis wanted, a part of her mind warned. When her guard was down he would pounce like the good attorney he was, and she would be totally defenceless without the barriers he had dismantled.

'I almost forgot,' she said much later. 'Thanks for the roses, they were beautiful.'

'You're beautiful,' he said, his voice as much a caress as the fingers that slid beneath her hair to stroke the nape of her neck gently.

'Jarvis, don't!' she pleaded, leaning away from him to escape those unexpected shivers of pleasure that raced through her.

'Don't what?' he smiled ironically. 'Don't tell you you're beautiful, or don't touch you?'

'Both!'

'That's going to be rather difficult,' he told her. 'I'm accustomed to speaking my mind, and since I saw you again at my mother's funeral I've been wanting to touch you in any and every possible way.'

Her cheeks went pink with embarrassment, and she lowered her long, silky lashes as she rose to her feet to put a safer distance between them. He had been in her thoughts almost every waking moment during the past two days, but his words struck a chord that awakened a fear in her.

'Don't play games with me, Jarvis,' she begged without turning to face him. 'I have neither the desire nor the experience for it.'

She had not heard him get up to follow her, but she felt him behind her, and his hands were firm and warm on her shoulders when he turned her to face him.

'I'm well past the stage of wanting to play games,' he assured her with a vibrant note in his voice that quickened her pulse.

His warm mouth shifted over hers to explore, taste and savour her lips with a featherlight sensuality to which she responded with a growing excitement. A tremor raced through her body, leaving in its wake a melting warmth that made her lean against him weakly with her hands sliding up along his broad back to cling to his wide shoulders.

Gina's mind felt drugged, and his sensual kisses aroused an aching longing that surged through her to sharpen on desire when his hands moulded her more firmly to the hard curve of his male body. He kissed her eyes, her cheeks, her throat, and she was too hopelessly lost to realise that he was easing down the zip of her dressing-gown when he held her a little away from him. It was only when his hands cupped the swell of her breasts that she realised what he had done, but the unexpected pleasure of his touch sent a jerky little sigh past her lips. The exciting, probing caress of Jarvis's fingers felt so right it could not be wrong, but that was where the danger lay, and it was with this sobering thought that she pulled away from him to zip up her dressing-gown with trembling fingers.

'No, Jarvis!' she protested huskily when he would have pulled her back into his arms. 'I think it's time you went home.'

There was a gleam of mockery in his eyes when he slid a lazy, sensual finger across her flushed cheek. 'Will you have dinner with me Tuesday evening?'

'I'd like that,' she accepted his invitation, and the smile that curved his sensuous mouth made her breath catch in her throat.

'I'll pick you up at seven,' he said, kissing her lightly on the lips and walking away from her to collect his jacket. 'Goodnight, my sweet.'

My sweet? If that was an endearment, then it sounded quite alien on his lips, and Gina stood with a bemused expression on her face long after Jarvis had let himself out.

Jarvis did not take Gina to Vittorio's for dinner on Tuesday evening. He took her instead to a place where the intimacy of the atmosphere made her feel as if they were the only people in the small restaurant. They talked throughout dinner, exchanging opinions and ideas about certain things, and sometimes arguing a point of interest.

'I missed you, Gina,' he said when they were drinking their coffee, his eyes mocking and probing simultaneously when they met hers. 'Did you miss me?'

She thought of how the hours had dragged for her until he had picked her up at her flat earlier that evening, but she answered cautiously. 'I have looked forward to this evening very much.'

'Then you did miss me?'

'Yes, I did,' she admitted before she could prevent herself.

'Ah!' he smiled triumphantly, leaning back in his chair to study her with mocking eyes. 'I'm very glad to hear that.'

'There are times when I don't like you very much, and this happens to be one of them.' She tried very hard to look annoyed, but the corners of her mouth quivered into a smile which could not be suppressed. 'You have a diabolical way of making me say things I have no intention of saying at all!'

His heavy eyebrows rose above mocking, vaguely accusing eyes. 'Is it so terrible to tell the truth?'

'No,' she answered gravely, 'but a girl ought to keep a man guessing instead of blurting out the truth at the least provocation.'

His smile faded as he leaned towards her across the table, and his hand captured hers unexpectedly. 'Will you come with me to Eldorado?'

'Eldorado?' she echoed, his touch almost as disconcerting as his query. 'Why do you want to go to Eldorado, and why at this time of night?'

'I have a sudden yen to visit my home,' he explained. 'And you haven't been there since my mother passed away, have you?'

'No, I haven't.' Her fingers trembled slightly in his, and she swallowed hard. 'I couldn't bear the thought of going to Eldorado knowing that she wouldn't be there.'

'Then come with me now.'

The thought of visiting Eldorado with Jarvis did not conjure up those fearful feelings she had had at the thought of going there on her own, and she nodded. 'I'll go with you.'

Eldorado was in darkness when they turned into the sweeping, circular drive and, caught in the powerful beams of the Jaguar, it was a magnificent, if somewhat sad, sight to behold. The servants would no doubt have kept it in order, but it seemed inanimate without Evelyn Cain there to breathe life into it. The two-storeyed house was etched sombrely against the night sky when they ascended the shallow steps on to the pillared portico, and a little shiver raced up Gina's spine when Jarvis produced a key to unlock the heavy oak door. It swung open on oiled hinges beneath his hand, and he stepped inside to switch on the light in the hall while Gina remained on the doorstep, her eyes wide and dark in a face that had gone strangely white. It would take time to find joy in remembering.

Jarvis turned to look at her, and his mouth tightened at what he saw. He held out his hand to her in silence, and there was comfort in the clasp of his strong, warm fingers about hers when he drew her inside and closed the door against the chill of the autumn night. He led her into the living-room and switched on the lights. Everything was as Gina remembered it. The gleam of polish on the wood of the furniture, the comfortably padded sofa and antique chairs arranged around the stone fireplace, and the wine-red velvet of the curtains at the windows. The three weeks since Aunt Evelyn's death might not have been. Nothing had been altered, everything was exactly the way her aristocratic godmother had preferred it, and Gina could almost make herself believe that at any moment Evelyn would walk into the living-room with that warm, welcoming smile creasing her lined face.

'Would you like a sherry?'

Jarvis's query startled her back to the reality of the present, and she was quivering in every limb as if from cold when she turned to see him opening the doors of the tall mahogany cupboard in the corner. 'Thank you, that would be nice.'

She watched the golden-brown liquid being poured into two crystal glasses, and Jarvis's eyes narrowed to discerning slits when her trembling fingers closed about the stem of the glass he offered her. He crossed the room to stand in front of the fireplace beneath the magnificent painting of a fox-hunt in progress, and his eyes were watchful as he gestured her towards a chair. But she could not sit down: she had a sudden, crazy desire to run like the fox in the painting. Instead, she wandered about the room, sliding her fingers lightly over the furniture while she sipped her sherry, welcoming its steadying influence.

'I've always loved this old house.' She broke the strained silence between them, her fingers absently exploring the intricate carvings in the backrest of the chair her godmother had favoured, and her sweeping glance encompassing the living-room from its beamed ceiling down to the Persian rugs covering the polished floor. 'Each room has such exquisite character,' she continued thoughtfully, 'but it's a house that needs to be lived in . . . and laughed in.'

The latter had been sadly lacking for many years, but perhaps some day . . . when Jarvis lost his aversion to marriage . . . and there were children . . . ! An unexpected stab of pain brought tears to her eyes, but she blinked them away hastily.

'Would you like to live here?' Jarvis's deep voice cut across her thoughts, and her fingers stilled their exploration of the rose carved into the wooden back-rest of a chair.

'I couldn't possibly do that.'

'If you married me we could live here together.'

Her heart leapt wildly in her breast, but her logical mind warned that it would be a mistake to take him seriously, and she donned a rigid, expressionless mask to hide her inner torment when she turned to face him. 'Don't be silly, Jarvis.'

He raised a quizzical eyebrow. 'Does the thought of marrying me not appeal to you?'

Gina was not sure how to deal with a situation such as this. Should she take him seriously and risk his mockery, or should she play safe and laugh it off? She did neither. Her anger rose sharply to dictate her actions, and her annoyance was clearly evident in her husky voice when she placed her empty glass on the low table beside her. 'This is a ridiculous conversation!' she told him.

'I'm serious, Gina.' He pushed himself away from the mantelpiece and his glass followed hers down on to the table. His features were stern, and there was no sign of mockery in the eyes that held hers for inter-minable seconds before he lowered his gaze to that pulse at the base of her throat which was so clearly conveying her distress. 'Marry me, and live here with me as my wife.'

'Stop it, Jarvis!' she ordered sharply, desperate now to bring to an end a situation that was developing into something painfully beyond her control. 'Don't talk about marriage when I happen to know that it's the last thing you want, and I'm beginning to wish you'd find someone else to entertain yourself with until Lilian Ulrich returns from her overseas trip!'

The height and breadth of him dominated her when he stepped towards her with an angry gesture of dismissal. 'If you think I find this entertaining, then you're mistaken. I asked you to marry me, and I expect an answer.'

The ensuing silence was fraught with a tension that seemed to emanate from Jarvis more than herself, and into this silence came the sound of the clock on the mantelpiece chiming eleven. Her nerves objected to that musical reminder of the time. It jarred and made her wince inwardly, and finally there was blessed silence once again. She was aware of Jarvis observing her intently, waiting for her to say something, but she had no intention of prolonging the conversation.

'Take me home, please,' she said icily, picking up her wrap and handbag, but they were removed from her hands as if her fingers had been deprived of the strength to hold on to them.

'Later,' he said, pulling her into his arms and setting his hard mouth purposefully on hers.

There had been no warning so that Gina could make an attempt at avoiding that fierce embrace, and consequently there had been not one iota of resistance in her body when she found herself moulded to his muscular frame. Neither was there any question of not responding; it came as naturally as breathing, and the searing passion of his kisses lit an answering fire in her which she could not have checked even if she had wanted to. Her slender body yielded with a trembling expectancy beneath his skilful hands, and her lips moved against his with a hunger that made her wish this moment would never end. His fiery mouth trailed explosive little kisses along her throat to her shoulder, and she could not suppress the shudder of pleasure that shook through her.

His hand worked its way through her hair until her scalp tingled with the touch of his fingers, and her eyes, stormy now with aroused passion, did not waver from his smouldering glance. 'You do love me, don't you, Gina?'

'Yes . . . oh, yes!' she admitted without hesitation or sense of shame. There was no point in shutting her mind to the obvious truth. She had fallen in love with him as a child and, despite her attempts to overcome it, she had never stopped loving him.

'Marry me, Gina,' he murmured, his lips exploring the smooth line of her jaw, and a bone-melting weakness invaded her body.

She had lost the power to think clearly, and the answer she gave came straight from her heart. 'If you really mean it, then yes . . . I'll marry you, Jarvis.'

CHAPTER FIVE

GINA was seated next to Jarvis at the centre of the long stinkwood table in Eldorado's main dining-room. She lowered her gaze to the plain gold band that had joined her engagement ring on her finger, and still found it difficult to believe that Jarvis had actually relinquished his much desired freedom to make her his wife.

There had been times during the past three weeks of hectic preparation when she had paused to wonder if she had not been too hasty in accepting his proposal, and whether they were not rushing into something they might both regret, but she had never voiced her misgivings to Jarvis. In his presence they had seemed so unimportant, so absurd, and she had repeatedly shrugged them aside.

Their wedding had been a very private ceremony which they had shared with family, and a few close friends whom they had invited to join them afterwards at Eldorado for a reception in the form of a luncheon party. They were a jovial group of people seated around the table, eating, and drinking champagne, and Gina's glance skipped across several unfamiliar face before it settled on Harold Ashton. The lawyer was looking rather more austere than when she had been called to his office to learn about the legacy her godmother had left her, but she did not pause to wonder at the reason for his expression as her glance shifted on to Clifford and Susan. They were holding hands and smiling at each other, perhaps at the memory of their own wedding day, and seated close

to them was her father, Raymond Osborne. There had
been a moistness in his eyes when he had taken her
into the church, and even now, as she thought about
it, it brought a lump to her throat.

Gina distanced herself from them all for a moment
to look at Jarvis. Her glance lingered on the strong
line of his jaw, and the stern yet sensuous mouth. She
had never imagined she could love a man with such
intensity, and it frightened her to some extent to know
that she had placed herself in such a vulnerable position. He turned his head then as if he had sensed her
appraisal, and, when their glances collided, she
glimpsed an expression in his eyes that gave rise to a
vague uneasiness which she could not explain. That
look was gone the next instant to be replaced by his
now familiar mocking smile, and her pulses raced as
if his smile was the key to her heart's mechanism.

The luncheon over, their guests moved on into the
living-room and out on to the terrace, and soon it was
time for Gina to change out of her wedding dress.
Susan went upstairs with her to help her out of the
heavy white satin and tulle dress, and then Gina was
left alone to change into the outfit she had spent so
much time selecting for their flight to Durban. It was
a long-sleeved dress with a wide collar, and the rich,
creamy colour of the soft woollen material was broken
by flecks of green that matched her eyes. The single
string of pearls about her throat had been a wedding
gift from Jarvis, and she had removed the combs from
her hair to let it hang free down to her shoulders.

Gina stared at her reflection in the mirror of Eldorado's guest-room with its eighteenth-century furniture,
and was satisfied with what she saw. The simple cut
of the dress made her look elegant and sophisticated,
but she did not linger long enough in front of the
mirror to notice the glow of happy serenity on her
face.

She was anxious to return to Jarvis, and to feel his presence close to her, but when she stepped into the hall, she found herself staring in startled recognition at the woman emerging from the living-room.

'Well, how fortuitous that I've been granted the opportunity to meet the bride!' Lilian Ulrich exclaimed in a musical, slightly accented voice. Her shimmering black dress clung to every seductive curve of her body to accentuate the alabaster smoothness of her pale skin. Her crimson lips were curved in a pleasant smile, but there was a coldness in her blue eyes that sent an unexpected shiver racing up Gina's spine. 'I flew in from Madrid this morning, and when I heard the news of your wedding I simply had to take a drive out to this quaint old home Jarvis had told me so much about.'

Her answer to Gina's unspoken query did not ease the tension which was taking a vicelike grip on every muscle in her body, and a warning flashed through her mind. This woman was her enemy, and it would be wiser to recognise the fact than to ignore it.

'Have you seen Jarvis?' she asked, her voice as deceptively calm as her appearance.

'I saw him briefly before he was forced to closet himself in the study with that dreary Harold Ashton, but I'm glad I have this opportunity to speak to you to tell you that I think you've made a terrible mistake.' Lilian Ulrich's smile did not waver, but her eyes were as cold as the frost so often in evidence of a cold winter morning. 'I have known Jarvis for quite some time, and if you perhaps have a silly notion that he's married you because he loves you, then you can forget it. He doesn't know the meaning of the word, for the simple reason that sentimentality has never featured largely in his life. As an attorney he deals with cold, harsh facts, and as a man he lives very much by a brutal, but realistic code. Jarvis is not by nature the

marrying kind. He never has been, and he never will
be, so I suggest you delve a little deeper elsewhere for
the cause of this sudden desire to tie himself up into
that matrimonial knot he's always despised. It could
be,' Lilian added with a cynical smile, 'that he stood
to gain something by marrying you, but only you will
know the answer to that.'

A cold hand seemed to clutch at Gina's heart. 'I
think you've said quite enough, and since you're here
as an uninvited guest, I would like to suggest that you
leave at once.'

'I was leaving anyway,' Lilian Ulrich smiled cynically, her glance sweeping up and down the length of
Gina's frozen body, 'but don't forget that I did warn
you.'

She left the house immediately, but her heady
perfume lingered in the hall as a reminder of her
presence, and Gina felt herself shaking. No matter
which way she looked at it, there had been a frightening ring of truth in everything Lilan had said. Jarvis
was not the marrying kind. Aunt Evelyn had said so
before her death, but no one could have put it across
as strongly as Lilian Ulrich who had known him for
some time. Jarvis was a man who had always made it
clear that he enjoyed his freedom. Why, then, this
sudden desire to bind himself in marriage? Was it
because he loved her? Gina wished she could answer
that query in the affirmative, but she had to be honest
with herself. Jarvis had never once used the word love,
but, until this day, she had believed he cared sufficiently. Now she was no longer so sure of that.

'Oh, damn that woman!' she muttered fiercely. 'She's
trying to cause trouble, and I'm not going to let her
succeed!'

She made a desperate attempt to shake off the spark
of uneasiness Lilian had aroused, and walked purposefully towards the study. Her hand was reaching to

open the door when she changed her mind and let it drop nervously to her side. Jarvis was not alone, Harold Ashton was with him, and Gina could hear every muted word quite clearly although their voices were not raised. They were discussing a client when Harold Ashton had referred to Jarvis. It was a very private conversation, but, as Gina turned to leave, she heard the lawyer question Jarvis about something which left her rooted to the spot.

'Does your wife know about that clause in your mother's will?'

Go! Leave now! Gina felt as if a siren had gone off in her mind, but her limbs refused to funtion. They were discussing something that concerned her. She did not want to hear it, but she somehow waited with bated breath for Jarvis's reply.

'I haven't told her yet.'

That deep, well-modulated voice was cold and forbidding, but Harold Ashton had obviously not been deterred by it.

'I think it was foolish of you to have hidden the truth from her, if you'll pardon me for saying so,' the lawyer remarked calmly, and Jarvis uttered an expletive that made Gina flinch.

'I wasn't going to jeopardise my future, and Eldorado's, by confronting Gina with that damned ridiculous clause in my mother's will!' Jarvis exploded harshly. 'God, my mother must have been out of her mind to make that stipulation that I had to marry Gina to inherit Eldorado!'

Gina felt that icy hand tightening about her heart, and the coldness spread swiftly until her entire body felt numb. *Oh, God, it's true!* Her mind screamed at her. *It's true!* Lilian Ulrich had been absolutely correct when she had intimated that Jarvis stood to gain something by marrying her. Aunt Evelyn had used

her as the key to Jarvis inheriting Eldorado, and Gina
was shattered by the discovery that her grandmother
could have been so cruel.

'Your wife has a right to know about it, Jarvis.'
Harold Ashton's voice intruded on her pain-filled
thoughts.

'I know that, dammit!' snapped Jarvis. 'But I'll tell
her in my own good time!'

Their voices grew distant, as if they were walking
towards the French windows that led out on to the
terrace, and Gina sagged limply against the wall when
shock sent a wave of terrible shudders rippling through
her body. She could feel the perspiration breaking out
on her cold forehead, and a wave of nausea rose inside
her which she had to suppress forcibly. She tried to
think clearly, but she failed, while she was consumed
with bitterness and the most unbearable pain. The
only thought engraved on her mind was the fact that
Jarvis had married her to inherit the home he loved
above all else. Jarvis would not marry anyone by
choice, Aunt Evelyn had said shortly before her death,
but he would do almost anything to get Eldorado.

'Oh, God!' Gina groaned softly. 'How could you
have done this to us, Aunt Evelyn?'

It was anger now that came to her rescue. It gave
her the strength to push herself away from the wall,
and when she turned, she saw Susan walking hurriedly
towards her.

'Gina, you look lovely!' her sister-in-law exclaimed
before her glance registered that Gina's face was
unusually pale. 'You're not going to be ill on your
wedding day, are you?'

Laughter drifted towards them from the living-
room, it mocked her for her blind stupidity, and she
wanted to be physically ill, but she pulled herself
together sharply.

'It's been a hectic couple of weeks,' she explained away her appearance. 'Where's my father?'

'He's out on the terrace with Cliff,' Susan replied, linking her arm affectionately through Gina's as they walked out of the house. 'I actually came to tell you that we must be on our way.'

'So soon?' Gina asked anxiously, reluctant to part with her family as they were the only safe harbour in this storm of misery into which she had suddenly been plunged.

'Yes, my dear.' Susan smiled and tapped a finger on her wristwatch. 'You may not have noticed, but it's almost time for you and Jarvis to leave for the airport.'

Gina could not bear to think of that as they stepped out on to the terrace. The sun was warm against her skin, but inside she felt like a block of ice. She went into her father's arms and clung to him with a fervour he must have found curious, but he was solid, he was there . . . and he loved her!

'All the best, my girl.' He smiled down at her.

'Thanks, Dad.' She tried to smile back at him, but his dear, smiling face became blurred as unexpected tears filled her eyes, and she hid her face against his jacket sleeve. 'Oh, Daddy!' she whispered in a muffled voice.

'Tears aren't such a bad thing, providing they're tears of happiness,' Raymond Osborne observed with a touch of humour some moments later when she had controlled herself and wiped away her tears with his handkerchief.

Gina nodded without looking at her father. How could she tell him that she had made a terrible mistake? How could she explain that she had been duped into this marriage, and that her gullible heart had led her to believe that Jarvis loved her as much as she loved him?

'Leaving already?' Jarvis spoke directly behind her when she was saying goodbye to Clifford and Susan, and her nerves reacted violently to his presence.

'I'm afraid so, Jarvis,' Clifford announced, gripping Jarvis's hand briefly. 'It's about time you left as well.'

Jarvis glanced at his watch and Gina stiffened when he placed a casual arm about her waist. 'Yes, we'll have to leave shortly if we're to be in time for our flight.'

Clifford laughed and jerked a thumb over his shoulder in the direction of the living-room. 'Your guests don't appear to be in a hurry to leave.'

'I'll get rid of them, don't worry,' Jarvis announced firmly.

Yes, Jarvis would get rid of them, Gina thought cynically when she stood watching her family drive away. Jarvis was very good at getting whatever he wanted, and he did so regardless of who got she stood watching her family drive away. Jarvis was very good at getting whatever he wanted, and he did so regard-less of who got hurt in the process.

The Boeing sped across the runway and rose into the sky like a gigantic bird with its silver wings spread out in flight. Gina's hands were clenched tightly in her lap and her body was tense, but her tension had nothing to do with a fear of flying. Jarvis sat next to her, his tall, magnificent body relaxed, and she wished, not for the first time, that she had not overheard that conversation between him and Harold Ashton. She had wanted to run, to end this marriage before it could begin, but the thought of having to face her family with the embarrassing and humiliating truth was something she had found unbearable even to contemplate. It was something which would have to remain between Jarvis and herself.

'You're tired and tense,' said Jarvis, his hand reaching for hers to uncurl her fingers in her lap.

'Lean back and close your eyes. We have an hour's flight ahead of us before we reach Durban.'

Gina did not argue, she did as she was told, but she could not relax no matter how she tried. Her mind was like a computer punching out information she had ignored before, and waves of pain washed over her repeatedly, forcing her to face the truth at last. She fingered her rings, and the final humiliation was like the thrust of a heated sword penetrating deep into her soul. Jarvis had never once said that he loved her. He had made very sure of her feelings, but he had kept his own carefully concealed. She had doubted him often enough, but loving him meant that she had to trust him, and she squirmed inwardly at the memory of how embarrassingly transparent he must have found her.

What was she going to do? Should she confront him with what she knew, or should she wait until he saw fit to tell her? Did she love him enough to keep up the pretence while knowing that he had married her solely to get his hands on Eldorado?

She turned her head slightly and observed Jarvis through lowered lids. He was reading a newspaper he had bought at the airport, and his stern, attractive profile sent a renewed stab of pain through her. Oh, how she hated him for doing this to her! She hated him so much that——Her throat tightened and stinging tears blurred her vision. She turned her face towards the window and kept her eyes tightly closed while she fought for control. To be truthful, she could never hate him entirely. She loved him despite everything, and . . . oh, God, how it hurt! It hurt to know that she had been failed by two people whom she had loved and trusted implicitly. Knowing and understanding Evelyn's fears, Gina could almost find it in her heart to forgive her godmother, but Jarvis's role in this hateful charade was totally unforgivable. He had been so diabolically clever in snaring her that she felt sickenedto the core at her own stupidity.

Could she go through with this marriage? was the question that leapt repeatedly into her mind. Dared she hope that by feigning ignorance she might somehow succeed in winning his love?

If you have some silly notion that he's married you because he loves you, then you can forget it. He doesn't know the meaning of the word. Gina had attempted to brush aside Lilian's remark as pure jealousy, but now it cut deep.

Refreshments were served on the flight. Gina was not hungry, but she forced herself to eat and drink to prevent Jarvis from suspecting that something was wrong. He spoke to her and she answered him, but she could not recall afterwards what either of them had said, and they had finally lapsed into a merciful silence. Jarvis may have sensed that she was not in a talkative mood, or perhaps he had preferred not to talk in order to brood about that conversation he had had with his mother's lawyer. She could not be sure.

Your wife has a right to know about it, Jarvis, Harold Ashton had said, and Jarvis had replied harshly, *I know that, dammit, but I'll tell her in my own good time.*

When had he planned to tell her? Tomorrow, after their marriage had been consummated and she had committed herself completely? The day after that? Or in a few months' time perhaps, when she would be too besotted with him to care?

A slow anger began to simmer inside Gina until it overrode the pain. He had laid a trap for her and she had walked into it like a trusting fool. He had made a mockery of her feelings. How dared he?

Jarvis had arranged for a hired car to be at their disposal when they arrived at the Louis Botha airport in Durban, and he took the north coast road to a fashionable hotel overlooking the rugged coastline. When they reached their destination late that afternoon a uniformed attendant appeared as if from nowhere to park their car and take care of their luggage while they entered the hotel.

Gina felt Jarvis's hand beneath her elbow when they ascended the shallow steps into the foyer, and the cool elegance she encountered was almost breathtaking. Persian rugs lay scattered across the black and white tiled floor, and attractive wrought-iron railings adorned the carpeted stairs winding up to the floor above. Strategically placed pot plants, original landscape paintings and ornamental mirrors induced an air of complete relaxation, and the two floral arrangements on the desk at reception added a dash of festivity to the atmosphere.

Jarvis signed the register while their suitcases were brought in, and then they were in the lift which was taking them up to the seventh floor. Gina felt her throat tighten the moment they were alone in the small lounge with its white and sun-yellow furnishings. She pushed open the white, panelled door leading out of the lounge, and Jarvis followed her into the spacious bedroom where a touch of gilt broke the stark white of the décor.

He glanced about him and raised a mocking eyebrow. 'It has a virginal appearance, wouldn't you say?' he observed.

Less than four hours ago Gina might have laughed and blushed a little, but the most she could manage at that moment was a tight smile.

'I imagine this is what's known as the honeymoon suite.'

His low rumble of laughter was abrasive to her raw nerves, and she avoided the hand that reached for her to walk into the adjoining bathroom. She closed the door behind her, shutting Jarvis out, and only then did she relax her guard for a moment. She raised her glance to find herself staring at her image in the mirror above the basin, and the eyes that met hers were shadowed with pain and misery. 'God, help me,' she prayed softly. 'What am I going to do?'

Jarvis glanced at her frowningly when she emerged from the bathroom some minutes later, but he said nothing. He had taken off his jacket and loosened his tie, but with a start of surprise, she saw him light a cigarette and turn to stare out of the window overlooking the ocean. She had never known him to smoke before and it made her wonder. Was his conscience troubling him? No, her mind punched out the answer cynically. Jarvis Cain was too arrogantly self-assured to be bothered with a conscience.

The sun had set on Gina's wedding day in more ways than one, and her future seemed as dark as the night outside. They freshened up and went down to dinner, but it was Jarvis who kept the conversation flowing between them rather than Gina. It was incredible, but she was torn between two equally strong desires: the desire to touch him, and the desire to lash out at him with all the pain and fury locked away inside her. For the moment, however, she could do neither. She could only stare at him when he was not looking, and wish with all her heart that it could have been different.

A terrible suspicion entered her tormented mind. Had that unexpected legacy been her godmother's way of apologising for what she had known would happen as a result of that clause she had inserted in her will? The thought was too painfull to dwell on, but Gina could not eradicate it completely from her mind.

It was still comparatively early when they returned to their suite, and Jarvis allowed her the use of the bathroom with a mocking gallantry while he lingered in the lounge. Thank God! she thought, her panic subsiding. He thinks I'm a nervous, jittery bride.

Gina showered and changed into the blue, diaphanous nightgown she had bought especially for her wedding night. *Her wedding night!* Those words echoed through her mind with a painful ring of irony, and she winced visibly. She caught sight of herself in the dressing-table mirror and, deciding that her night attire was far too revealing, pulled on her silk dressing-gown in a matching colour and tied the belt firmly about her slender waist before brushing her hair vigorously to rid herself of some of her aggression. She was also nervous and had to brace herself before she walked out of the bedroom to confront Jarvis, but despite her efforts, her knees threatened to buckle beneath her when she stepped into the dimly lit lounge.

'I ordered a bottle of champagne,' Jarvis said while his thumb eased the cork out of the bottle's neck. It shot out, making her jump as if a pistol had been fired unexpectedly at close range, and she stared almost hypnotically while he poured the sparkling liquid into two tall glasses. He placed one in her hand and lifted his own in salute. 'Let's drink to our future together, Gina.'

He raised his glass to his lips, his steel-grey eyes holding hers with that hint of mockery in their depths, and a renewed wave of near physical pain washed over her. Until that moment she had almost succeeded in convincing herself that she could go through with it, but she knew now that it would be impossible.

Afraid that her glass might slip from her trembling fingers, she placed it hurriedly on the glass-topped table and turned her back on him to stare blindly out of the window.

'I can't drink to our future together.'

She had not meant to say that, but the words had somehow been torn from her, and she heard the clink of his glass on the glass-topped table before he came to her side.

'What's the matter, Gina?'

His hands were gentle on her shoulders when he turned her to face him, but his gentleness merely set fire to that spark of anger she had been nursing inside her for some hours, and she shrugged herself free to take a pace away from him.

She stared at him through a mist of pain and anger which she had difficulty in hiding, and her glance rested for a moment on those powerful shoulders straining against the expensive silk of the white shirt which he had unbuttoned almost to his waist. Dark hair curled against his tanned, muscular chest, and her fingers tingled with an unbidden desire to touch him. Her body's treachery angered her, and green fire leapt in her eyes when she met and held his steady, probing gaze.

'I know why you married me, Jarvis, so there's no longer any need for you to pretend.' Her husky voice was brittle with the effort involved to hide her pain and misery. 'I went downstairs to look for you after I'd changed out of my wedding dress, and I heard you talking to Harold Ashton in the study.'

His eyes narrowed perceptibly, but his expression remained unaltered, and during the brief, ensuing silence only the sound of the waves crashing against the rocks could be heard through the open window.

'I see,' he spoke into the silence while she searched in vain for some sign of remorse in his granite-hard features. 'I must admit that I'm relieved to hear that, but I can explain if you'll let me.'

'Oh, I'm sure you can explain it all,' she said coldly. 'You're a brillant attorney, and I have no doubt that your defence strategy would be planned down to the very last detail, but in this instance you could have spared yourself the time you spent preparing it.'

'Don't be an idiot, I——'

'Don't touch me!' Her eyes were twin fires of anger
in her pale, pinched face when she shrank from the
hands reaching out to her. 'You lied to me, you made
me believe you cared, but all the time it was Eldorado
you really wanted. And it was such an easy victory,
wasn't it? Drawing from your vast experience with
women I imagine you took one look at me and knew
exactly what a gullible fool I would be. I'll make the
little idiot fall in love with me, and from then on it'll
be easy. Marriage to me would not only place Eldorado
safely within your reach, it would give you access to
my bed if and when you found you were too tired to
go out looking for it elsewhere. Isn't that what you
thought? Oh, I'll bet it was!'

'Now, look here, I——'

'You played your part so well, Jarvis, but I despise
you for it, and I could almost hate your mother for
doing this to me,' she continued sarcastically, punishing
herself more than him. 'For God's sake, Jarvis, why
didn't you tell me about that stipulation in your
mother's will?'

'Would you have married me had you known?'

'Most certainly not!' she snapped, and a smile of
devilish satisfaction curved his mouth.

'That's exactly why I didn't tell you.'

Gina drew a shuddering breath and shook her head
in a visible attempt to clear her mind. 'You've turned
our marriage into an embarrassing and humiliating
farce, and I can't go through with it.'

'I'm afraid I can't let you back out now, Gina.' He
gestured her to silence when she would have interrupted him. 'My mother's will stipulates that we have
to stay married for a year before I can lay claim to
Eldorado as my rightful inheritance, and I have every
intention of complying with her wishes, ridiculous as
they may be.'

She was trapped, trapped into the marriage she had wanted so very much, but which she now found abhorrent. Frustration and resentment mingled to sharpen her anger. 'Damn you, Jarvis! I don't want to remain married to you under these circumstances!'

'I can't give you your freedom,' he stated flatly. 'It's become a question of honour.'

'Honour!' she snorted disparagingly. 'There was nothing honourable about what you did, so don't make me laugh!'

'An annulment would be an embarrassment to both of us, and I believe you're aware of that or you wouldn't have been here now. You're legally my wife, Georgina, and that's how it's going to stay for the next year.'

Legally his wife! She had not wanted to be his wife merely in the legal sense. She had wanted to be his wife in every possible sense of the word, she had wanted to love and be loved, but her dream had been shattered into tiny, agonising fragments, and she blamed her godmother for this as much as she blamed Jarvis.

'If I have to stay married to you, then it will be a marriage in name only,' she insisted bluntly.

'You called our marriage a farce,' he reminded her harshly. 'Do you want it to be an even greater farce?'

She glared up at him furiously and hissed, 'If you think I'd let you come near me now, then you're mistaken!'

'We shall see about that!'

Alerted by the unrelenting set of his lean jaw and that flesh of icy anger in his eyes, Gina turned and fled into the bedroom. Her heart was racing in her throat, almost choking her when she tried to slam the door behind her, but Jarvis's shoulder was there, and he was applying a pressure that her puny strength could not cope with.

'There's no point in trying to escape the inevitable, my dear Georgina.' He smiled somewhat satanically when he finally stepped into the room and closed the door behind him.

She heard the scrape of metal against metal, but she paid no attention to it as she backed several paces away from him. 'If you so much as lay a finger on me I shall never forgive you!'

'I usually get what I want,' he warned ominously, thrusting his hands into his pockets and trailing his insolent glance down the length of her trembling body.

'Not this time!' she argued fiercely.

'Do you want to bet on that?'

'Don't touch me!' she told him furiously, backing away again when his hands emerged from his pockets. But she found herself up against the dressing-table with Jarvis lessening the distance between them in one long stride.

It felt as if her body had become one wild, throbbing pulse when he paused less than a pace away from her. The scent of his woody cologne on his heated body was a potent mixture which attacked her senses, and she knew a desperate, unbidden longing that sent a bone-melting weakness surging through her. She knew she had to fight it, but she also knew it was a battle she would lose if he touched her. Jarvis was observing her intently, his steely eyes taking note of every expression that flitted across her pale, sensitive features, and his agile mind analysed it with the speed of a man accustomed to probing beneath the surface.

'You may think you hate me at this moment, but in truth you know you want me to touch you.'

'No!' There was an undisguised ring of panic in her raised voice at the accuracy with which he had summed up her feelings. 'No, that isn't true!'

He smiled derisively. 'Your lips may say no, Gina, but I don't have to touch you to know that your body is saying something quite the opposite.'

'Oh, for God's sake!' she cried out in helpless anger, and he laughed triumphantly as he walked away from her towards the bathroom.

'I suggest you give it some thought while I take a much-needed shower . . . and if you're contemplating running out on me,' he held up a key between his thumb and forefinger for her inspection, 'the bedroom door is locked.'

'You fiend!' she berated him fiercely, her hands clenched at the sides of her quivering body, but he merely laughed, and she could still hear him laughing for some time after he had closed the bathroom door behind him.

Gina paced the floor in a fury which was directed mainly at herself. She felt like a caged animal forced to await the arrival of a mate it did not want, but who it knew had the power to make it submit, and she despised herself for being so weak. She had never known that one could love and hate with equal intensity and, as a weapon in Jarvis's hands, either could be used to destroy her.

She stared at the enormous bed, and suddenly she wanted to cry. This was her wedding night, the start of a two-week honeymoon which she had imagined would be one of the happiest times of her life, but all that remained of that dream was a hurt that went so deep she believed nothing could assuage it. She was also trying to cope with a growing anxiety. She could not sleep on that bed with Jarvis. If he touched her she would be lost, and to surrender to him would be a humiliation too great to bear.

A large, comfortably padded armchair had been placed in a convenient and inviting position beside the window, and Gina saw it as a refuge. She curled herself up in it, and the cushions seemed to enfold her comfortingly to take the shape of her body. She

wanted to cry again, but she forced back the tears,
determined not to give Jarvis the satisfaction of
knowing that he had succeeded in making her weep.

CHAPTER SIX

GINA'S body tensed when she heard the bathroom door open. She did not want to look at Jarvis, but against her will her glance shifted in his direction. He was entering the room with a towel draped loosely about his lean hips, and his dark hair lay in damp disarray across his broad forehead.

'Not in bed yet?' he asked, raising an amused eyebrow, and her breath locked in her throat as she stared at his muscled chest and arms as he walked barefoot across the carpeted floor towards her.

She had always been intensely aware of that powerful aura of masculinity surrounding him, but at that moment he was exuding a raw maleness that made her senses leap wildly in response.

She looked away hastily, afraid that her eyes might convey her true feelings. 'I'll sleep in this chair, thank you,' she said stubbornly.

'Don't be ridiculous!' he laughed shortly, leaning over her to place his hands on the arms of the chair, and the clean, male smell of him trapped her into a helpless state of wanting.

She shrank from him against the cushions. 'Stay away from me, Jarvis!' she snapped.

'And if I don't?'

She raised her wary glance to his to see flames of desire igniting in his eyes, and was promptly reduced to a trembling mass of conflicting emotions which made her resort to begging in an attempt at self-preservation.ervation. 'Please, Jarvis!'

'I like the sound of that,' he smiled sensuously.

'Your sadistic mind would!'

He ignored her biting sarcasm, and his smouldering eyes burned down into hers with a probing intensity that frightened her. 'I want you, Georgina, and nothing is going to stop me from having you, since I happen to know that you want me too.'

'No!'

It was a cry of despair rather than a denial, and his mouth curved in a slow, mocking smile that made her cringe inwardly with embarrassment and self-disgust.

'Do you want me to believe you're trembling because you know you'll find my touch repulsive, Georgina?'

Nothing, she discovered, every escaped his notice, and her resentment erupted with an angry force. 'You're a fiend!' she choked.

A bored look entered his eyes as he straightened and turned from her to walk towards the mirrored dressing-table. 'You've said that before.'

'And I'll say it again,' she hissed at the muscles rippling in his broad back while he brushed his hair back severely. 'You're a fiend!'

'Because I have the ability to detect your weakness?' he demanded with an infuriating calmness when he put down the brush and turned to face her.

He was laughing at her; she could see it in that hint of amusement lurking in his eyes. They both knew that their desire for each other was an omnipotent force which they had had great difficulty in keeping tightly leashed during the weeks prior to their marriage, and it amused him now to see her futile battle against it.

'Oh, God!' she groaned helplessly, leaping agitatedly to her feet to stare blindly out of the window at the restless ocean lying shimmering in the moonlight.

She wished she could stop trembling, but most of all she wished she could feel anger rather than this numb acceptance of something she could not control.

Jarvis came up behind her, she could feel the warmth of his body against her back, and his hand reached out over her shoulder to tug at the sash that slid the curtain across the window. The rest of the world was abruptly shut out, and now there was only Jarvis and herself, and the heavy thudding of her treacherous heart.

A heavy strand of hair was lifted away from her neck, and his warm mouth brushed against her skin in a caress that awakened a thousand little nerves to the pleasure of his touch. His arms circled her waist, his hands tugging at the belt of her dressing-gown, and he lifted the silky garment off her shoulders to let it slither down her body until it lay in a crumpled heap at her bare feet. His fingers slid in a featherlight caress down her bare arms and up again to her shoulders, and Gina stood immobile, trapped by sensations her body welcomed even while her mind rejected them. The flimsy straps were stroked off her shoulders, and her diaphanous nightgown followed the same path as the dressing-gown. The only thing left between Jarvis and herself was the towel still draped about his hips, and Gina was beyond caring when his hands began their gentle exploration of her trembling body.

Don't let him do this to you! Her mind shouted it frantic command, but her trembling body had a mind of its own, and in this instance it was infinitely more powerful.

His hands trailed down along her smooth hips and shapely thighs, and up again across her taut, flat stomach until the weight of her small breasts rested in the palms of his strong hands. She closed her eyes, swaying back against him as she felt herself drowning in the pleasure sensations aroused by his thumbs moving back and forth across the hardened peaks of her breasts, but her mind was still clear enough to object.

'I—I want you to—to know, Jarvis,' she heard herself saying in a hoarse, halting voice which she could barely recognise as her own, 'that I—I hate and despise you for the—the heartless way you trapped me into this marriage, and if—if I live to—to be a thousand I shall—shall never, *ever* forgive you.'

He turned her into his arms, and the abrasiveness of his chest hair against her breasts increased her excitement. 'You may hate and despise me for as long as you wish, my beautiful Gina,' he murmured thickly against her throat, 'but the fact remains that you want me, and you can't deny it.'

'I shan't try to deny it again,' she confessed against her will, 'but I—I hope you'll be—be satisfied knowing that my body is all you're ever going to have.'

'I don't recall asking for more.' He thrust home the truth, and it was like a knife being twisted savagely in a raw, bleeding wound.

'That's true,' she whispered soberly, raising her eyes to his and finding nothing there except naked desire. 'The fault was mine alone for believing in something which was never there.'

Desire made way for an icy anger, and his hands tightened almost savagely about her waist as if he wanted to snap her slender body in half.

'Shut up!' he growled, and further speech was made impossible when his mouth swooped down on hers with a savage passion that seared her like fire.

Gina's mind was also silenced, she was drugged by his kisses into a state of euphoria, and afterwards she could never recall whether Jarvis had lifted her on to the bed she had dreaded so much, or whether she had lowered herself on to it with him. She was conscious only of his lips and hands exploring, and arousing her body until it seemed as if every hitherto hidden nerve

and sinew came alive with a quivering, aching desire
that cried out for fulfilment.

Initially she had had no intention of participating
in this act of making love, but a hungry yearning
erupted inside her. Her hands eagerly roamed his hard
body, and she was guided by instinct rather than
knowledge when the sensitive pads of her fingers
explored the taut, quivering muscles from his wide
shoulders down to his lean hips and hard thighs. His
breathing became laboured and uneven, and his
aroused body trembled against hers.

'God, I've longed for this!' he groaned, his knees
parting her soft thighs, and her slumbering mind was
suddenly awakened to the knowledge that she could
not give herself to this man who had tricked her into
marriage merely to claim his inheritance.

'Jarvis, no!' she gasped, attempting to push him
away from her in a fit of panic while her body writhed
beneath his to escape his possession. 'Please, I—I
can't!'

She was trapped beneath the weight of his body,
and he imprisoned her hands above her head to stare
with glazed eyes down into her flushed face. Her red-
gold hair lay in disarray across the pillow, and her
stormy eyes successfully hid the pain of knowing that,
for Jarvis, this would never be anything more than a
physical act of desire.

'You can and you will!' he insisted gratingly.

And she did!

Her heart and mind might have joined forces to cry
out their silent rejection, but her body was concerned
only with that aching need for something which it
could still only guess at.

Jarvis was surprisingly gentle in his possession of
her, as if he had known that she was still a virgin, but
that initial stab of pain made her desire plummet
briefly before it rose again to take on a new dimension.

Her heart seemed to still in her breast, and it felt as if
she could scarcely breathe while his hard, thrusting
body initiated her into a world of new, piercingly
sweet sensations. Her pleasure was intense, rising and
swelling inside her like a wave in a storm-tossed ocean.
She could not think, she could only feel, and she clung
helplessly to Jarvis, her arms and legs locking about
him while her body arched towards his and willed him
never to stop. She was trapped in a vortex of the most
exquisite sensations, which took control of her body,
dictating her actions in the rhythm of love and inten-
sifying her pleasure in the union of their bodies until
she almost cried out with the need to be released from
the aching, paradisical sweetness of it. His name
passed her lips on a jerky sigh when, at last, that near
intolerable tension snapped inside her, and she was
caught up in a wave of the most ecstatic pleasure that
left her tingling and trembling as it spread through
her body until every vital part of her was satisfied.
Jarvis groaned, shuddering as he sagged heavily on
top of her, and then there was only their ragged
breathing while their hearts raced in unison in the
aftermath of a passion shared.

They were lying beside each other in the now
darkened room, not touching each other while the
glow of rapture faded and sanity returned to bring
with it the stinging reality of her marriage. Hot tears
filled her eyes, and they spilled silently from her cheeks
on to her pillow. If she had made a sound, then she
was not aware of it, but something alerted Jarvis to
her distress, and he raised himself on one elbow to
lean over her in the darkness which was broken only
by the strip of moonlight filtering into the room
through the slight gap between the curtains.

'Gina?'

His hand touched damp cheek, but she brushed it
away angrily and rolled over to lie with her back

towards him. 'For pity's sake, leave me alone!' she croaked.

'As you wish,' he said in a voice which had become so cold and impersonal that it sent a fresh stab of pain through her.

Her tears flowed faster, but this time she stifled the sound of her weeping in the pillow. She hated Jarvis! She hated him! But she hated herself as well. She had been a fool to believe in his sincerity, but she was an even greater fool for still wanting him.

Gina did not sleep very well. She spent most of the night listening to the waves beat against the rocks, and the sound of Jarvis's deep, even breathing. This should have been the happiest night of her life, but instead it had become a nightmare. How was she going to survive this year ahead of her while knowing that Jarvis had married her solely to inherit Eldorado? What would he expect of her when that period drew to a close? Would he tell her to go, or would he ask her to stay?

Her mind was beginning to reel with one frantic thought after the other, and she somehow suspected that the nightmare was only just beginning.

It was a hot, humid morning. The rocky stretch of beach was ideal for fishermen, but unsafe for swimming and the hotel pool beckoned almost like an oasis in the desert. Jarvis had gone down earlier to secure a place for them on the smooth lawn surrounding the tiled pool, and Gina was relieved to have these few moments alone to herself in their suite. This was the last day of their honeymoon. It had been two weeks of recrimination and self-disgust, and Jarvis had not spared her for a moment. He had mocked her, and he had baited her. He had driven her to a peak of blinding fury which she had not known before, but he had also revealed to her some of the many exciting

facets of making love. Bitterness and resentment had
at times made her fight him like a wildcat. She would
scream abuse at him, but in the end she had always
surrendered humiliatingly to that driving, passionate
need he had aroused in her, and which would never
cease to make her feel ashamed of herself.

She blushed and cringed inwardly merely at the
thought of it when she put on her short, towelling
robe over her bikini and pushed her feet into low-
heeled sandals. The two weeks at the coast had been
glorious in one way. The sun had deepened the colour
of her skin to a creamy, golden tan which credited her
with a healthy appearance despite the shadows which
frequently lurked in her eyes.

It was not difficult to find Jarvis among the many
hotel guests sunbathing on the green, well-kept lawn
surrounding the pool area. He was lounging on a
recliner close to the pool when Gina joined him, and
she could not help noticing that his skin had tanned
to a deep ochre. Her glance trailed freely over his
muscular body in the snug-fitting bathing trunks, and
her heart skipped several thudding beats at the mere
pleasure of looking at him. An attractive blonde was
roasting her oiled body in the sun a short distance
from them and, despite Gina's presence, the blonde's
admiring glance seemed to be drawn repeatedly
towards Jarvis. *You may look as much as you want,
but he's mine!* It was a proud and strangely possessive
assertion that leapt unbidden into Gina's mind, but it
was also a sobering one. Jarvis would never be hers.
He belonged to himself, and perhaps also to Eldorado,
but he would never belong to her!

'Give me that,' he instructed, sitting up to take the
bottle of suntan lotion away from her, and pouring
some of the sweet-smelling liquid into the palm of his
hand.

He joined her on her recliner, seating himself behind her, and her body tensed when his fingers began to spread the protective lotion over her back. His touch was firm, almost therapeutic, and she felt her muscles relax slowly. She closed her eyes, finding joy in his ministrations, but his touch altered abruptly. The sensuality flowing unexpectedly from his fingers drew a lightning response from her that filled her with dismay, and her anger rose sharply.

'That's enough!' she snapped, turning to take the suntan lotion from him and twisting the cap on to the bottle.

'Stop hating yourself, Gina,' he mocked her, trailing his fingers in a morally destructive path down the hollow of her spine. 'It isn't a crime for a woman to want a man, and especially when that man happens to be her husband.'

'I wish you'd shut up!' she fumed in a lowered voice, jerking away from him. 'And don't touch me!'

'I'm afraid it's common knowledge that we're on our honeymoon,' he laughed softly, returning to his recliner, 'and I've warned you before that people would find it odd if we never touched each other in public.'

'Go to hell!'

'I think I'm beginning to like this wildcat side of your nature, Georgina.' He infuriated her with his unperturbed attitude. 'I happen to find you extremely attractive, and very desirable when you're bristling and hissing with anger and indignation.'

'Really?' she murmured sarcastically, adjusting the recliner and settling herself comfortably to relax in the sun.

'Do you suppose that when my mother wrote that clause into her will she might have known that I would find you irresistible?'

Her eyes were shooting darts of green fury when she turned her head to glare at him. 'She had no right to manipulate my life the way she did!'

'*Our* lives,' he corrected smoothly and somewhat cynically. 'My mother was a very headstrong woman, and she had the ability to make sure that she always got what she wanted. In that respect I am unfortunately very much like my mother.'

'I don't approve of what she did, but I can partly understand what had driven her to it.' It had taken almost two weeks to find a valid reason to forgive her godmother, but it might take an eternity to forgive Jarvis. 'Your mother desperately wanted to see you settled, and she was terribly afraid you might decide to marry someone whom she considered totally wrong for you.'

'Someone like Lilian Ulrich, perhaps?' he smiled derisively.

'Yes,' she confirmed in a whisper, the mention of that woman's name was enough to send a renewed shaft of pain through Gina, and Jarvis gestured disparagingly with his hand.

'There was never any danger of that. Lilian and I were quite content to play the game by the rules, and the rules excluded marriage.'

'That was something you should have told your mother,' Gina said accusingly, knowing in her heart that none of this would have happened if there had not been such a break in communication between Jarvis and Aunt Evelyn.

'Perhaps I should have,' Jarvis agreed mockingly, his eyes narrowed against the sun, 'but then I might never have made the effort to get to know you, and just think of all the excitement I would have missed out on.'

There was a painful ring of truth in his remark. He might not have made the effort to get to know her if it had not been for his mother's will, but she would have had so much less pain to endure if he had stayed out of her life altogether. Would there ever be an end to this agony she was going through? she wondered as she turned her head to glare at him once again.

'You're a callous, egotistical, and sadistic brute! You care only about the things *you* want in life, and it doesn't seem to bother you if anyone else gets hurt in the process!'

'Have I hurt you, Gina?' he asked blandly, but there was a blantant sensuality in the eyes that held hers. 'Have I hurt you at any time during these past two weeks?'

Her cheeks went hot with shame and anger. 'How typical of you to reduce everything we discuss to a physical level!'

'Isn't that what we've both been doing these past two weeks?' Jarvis struck back, and she drew a quick, strangled breath as if he had slapped her.

'Yes, damn you!' she shouted at him furiously, her knuckles whitening as she gripped the sides of her recliner to prevent herself from striking out at him physically. 'But a relationship is bound to peter out swiftly if it's based purely on a physical attraction, and I find that thought consoling.'

Jarvis smiled noncommittally, and his silence seemed to infuriate her more than any words could have done.

She closed her eyes against the blinding sunlight and tried to relax, but her mind gave her no peace. Jarvis had stormed into her orderly life, he had shattered the defences she had erected so carefully, and all she was left with was the painful knowledge that he had tricked her into giving him her heart while his was still free.

Gina left him asleep on the recliner some time later and went into the pool to cool off. She had it entirely to herself for a few minutes, and she swam a few lengths before she got out to get dry.

She was putting on her towelling robe when Jarvis opened one eye lazily. 'Where do you think you're going?'

'I'm going up to our suite to shower and change before lunch,' she answered sarcastically as she pushed her feet into her sandals. 'Any objections?'

'I'll come with you,' he announced, sitting up and pulling his T-shirt on over his head.

'I don't need you to hold my hand while I'm showering.'

'Ah, but you might need me for something else,' he smiled mockingly, picking up his beach towel and slinging it across one broad shoulder as he accompanied her across the lawn.

Her face flamed, and a suitable rebuke escaped her in her fury as she marched on ahead of him into the air-conditioned hotel.

She could not look at him in the lift. Her heart was beating in her throat, and she prayed that his remark had been made purely in jest, but when they entered their suite she knew that she had not misunderstood that look in his eyes.

He reached for her when they walked into the bedroom. She tried to avoid his hands, but they were all over her. Her towelling robe fell to the floor, her bikini was peeled rather roughly off her sun-heated body, and her inability to get away from him made her beat against his chest with her clenched fists.

'Leave me alone, Jarvis!' she cried desperately. 'Take your hands off me!'

'If the physical attraction is going to peter out as swiftly as you said, then we'd better make the best of it while it lasts.' He flung her own words back at her, lifting her naked body effortlessly and carrying her towards the bed.

Her efforts to escape were futile. He needed only one hand to imprison her arms against the pillows above her head, and his heavy thigh pinned the rest of her body to the bed while he discarded his T-shirt and bathing trunks. Her breath was rasping in her throat, and her eyes shot green fire at him, but her body quivered in shameful response when he trailed a sensually arousing hand along her hips and thighs and up again to cup one of her breasts. She groaned helplessly when his fingers expertly teased the pink nipple into a hard button of desire, and she could not withhold that husky cry of pleasure when his mouth continued the erotic arousal his fingers had begun.

Jarvis raised his head when her struggles desisted, and his smouldering eyes followed the path of his hand as it trailed over the feminine contours of her body to set fire to her blood. His fingers stroked her gently, intimately, and aroused a sharp, swift response that made her hips arch towards his with an invitation that prompted him to crush her against his own shuddering and aroused body.

'God, Gina, you're so beautiful, and I can't seem to get enough of you!'

His voice was low and vibrant, like the throaty growl of an animal staking his claim on his mate. It frightened and excited her, and the last fragment of her fragile resistance fled when his mouth devoured hers with a savage hunger that drove every vestige of thought from her mind.

There was no escape from this violent onslaught on Gina's emotions. She was defeated and swamped with feelings she could not control, and their bodies fused together in a seemingly endless, pagan rhythm which left them both drained, but physically sated.

'You're everything a man could ever wish for and more,' Jarvis murmured throatily a considerable time later while he slid a possessive, caressing hand along her relaxed body.

Gina might have been physically sated, but her mind was filled with discontent as she rolled away from him and got up to put on her towelling robe. 'I may be everything a man like yourself could wish for, but that feeling will last only until you tire of me.'

'Will you tire of me, Gina?' he questioned her with that stinging mockery she knew so well, and she glanced at him over her shoulder, her lowered lashes veiling her pleasure at the sight of his magnificent and superbly fit body reclining in unashamed nakedness on the bed.

'Yes,' she answered coldly and untruthfully. 'I have no doubt I shall tire of you eventually.'

Bitterness, disappointment and anger had prompted those words, but deep down inside her there was a nagging voice that cried out the contrary. Jarvis smiled, his eyes gleaming with mockery as if he had looked into her soul and discovered the answer to something she stubbornly ignored, and she hated him all the more for his keen and uncanny perception.

'I'm going to take a shower,' she said icily, but helpless tears filled her eyes as she marched into the bathroom and closed the door behind her.

Gina was wandering aimlessly through Eldorado's many rooms, switching on lights and switching them off again as she went. Jarvis had told her not to expect him home for dinner, he had an important meeting with a client, and he was going to be late. But she was restless and edgy on her own in that enormous house. She had always loved Eldorado. Its peace and tranquillity had always enfolded her like a warm blanket in winter, but now that was all gone. The rooms seemed cold and unfriendly, and she was beginning to hate it. Eldorado was the cause of her unhappiness. It stood between her and Jarvis like a secret lover, but Gina's feelings were far stronger than jealousy.

The past six weeks since their return from their honeymoon had been agonising for her. They had been to the farm twice, but the strain of having to be polite to Jarvis in front of her family had been intolerable, and she had refused to go again. Their only method of communication these days was through insults, mockery and sarcasm. It was as if they each kept a private score card to tally up their hits, and how often they could hurt each other. Life had become a battleground. She despised herself almost more than she despised Jarvis for what he had done to her, yet he had only to walk into the room and she would find herself aching for him.

It was despicable of her to want a man who did not love her. The torment of it nearly drove her out of her mind, and yet she could not help herself. The only time she felt truly alive was when he made love to her, and afterwards she would go through a private hell of her own. Her soul was being ripped to shreds, and with each tear something died inside her.

She had no one she could talk to, and no one whom she could ask for advice. Norman Thorpe was the only friend she had had, but their friendship had disintegrated when the news of her engagement to Jarvis had leaked out. She had realised then that Norman's feelings for her had gone far deeper than she had imagined, and she had decided it would be kinder to stay out of his way.

To make matters worse, she had begun to suspect that Jarvis was seeing Lilian Ulrich again. If this was true, then it was all being done very discreetly. No one could point a finger at them, not even Gina, but Lilian had been at every function they had attended during the past weeks, and the evenings when Jarvis did not arrive home until after dinner were becoming more and more frequent.

Gina went to bed eventually and tried to read a book to take her mind off her problems, but she had difficulty in concentrating. Was Jarvis with a client, or was he with Lilian? She writhed inwardly as she twisted the knife in her own heart. Oh, God, why did she have to torment herself like this?

She tried to read again, but without much success, and she was staring blankly at the printed pages at ten-thirty that evening when she heard Jarvis's car come up the drive. Her fingers tightened on the book, and tension seemed to take a grip on her lungs which made it difficult to breathe normally.

Jarvis walked into their bedroom quietly some minutes later, and his eyebrows rose in mild surprise at finding her awake. He looked tired, she thought, compassion softening her features as she lowered her glance to the shirt he had unbuttoned at his throat, and the dark grey suit jacket draped casually over his arm. But she cringed inwardly at the mockery in the eyes that met hers a moment later when he crossed the room and flung his jacket carelessly on to the chair beside the window.

'I'm flattered that you waited up for me, but I'm afraid I shall have to disappoint you this evening,' he mocked her cruelly, his glance resting insolently on the agitated rise and fall of her breasts beneath the lacy bodice of her nightgown. 'I'm going to take a shower, and then I have an important brief to work on which should keep me busy for another hour or so.'

'Do you have to reduce everything I do or say to a sexual level?' she demanded coldly, hating him for making her feel like a cheap wanton who had only one thought in mind—to get him into bed with her.

'Hasn't it ever occurred to you that there could be more to life than just sex?'

'Such as reading to pass the time until your husband gets home to your waiting arms?' he demanded cynically, removing the book from her hands to glance at the title and dropping it back into her lap. 'Reading is such a poor substitute for the passion you could experience in a man's arms, and you're a passionate woman, Georgina. In fact, you're quite the most passionate woman I've ever known.'

'And you *would* know, of course, since you have such a vast experience to draw your conclusions from,' she countered sarcastically, her fingers tightening about the book in an attempt to hide the fact that her hands were trembling.

'You have one fault, my dear wife,' he continued, ignoring her sarcasm. 'You enjoy sex, but you refuse to admit it. Instead of being proud of the pleasure your body can give and receive, you persist in behaving as if you've participated in something shameful.'

'Does that surprise you?' she demanded, shaking with pain and fury as she watched him strip off his shirt and fling it on the chair in a visible display of anger. 'Do you think I enjoy being the wife of a man who tricked me into marriage simply to claim his inheritance? Do you think I have cause to rejoice in the knowledge that I can find pleasure in your arms while I despise you for what you did?'

His mouth tightened as her verbal arrows found their mark, and his narrowed eyes glittered in the bedside light as he approached her where she sat propped up against the pillows on the old-fashioned four-poster bed.

'If you think I liked the idea of having my freedom curtailed by that crazy stipulation in my mother's will, then you're mistaken, but since I had no choice in the matter, it seems logical to me that we might as well make the best of it, and draw whatever enjoyment we can out of a situation which has become unpalatable to both of us.'

'That may be your solution to the problem, but it isn't mine!' she hissed up at him furiously.

'Oh, come now, Georgina,' he laughed harshly. 'You're an intelligent, attractive, and very desirable woman. Did you expect me to live under the same roof with you for a year without touching you? That would be defying the laws of nature, don't you think?'

He strode into the bathroom and closed the door behind him, leaving her fuming inwardly at her inability to find a suitable answer.

What *was* there to say? she wondered rationally when she had calmed down a little. Most of what he had said was true, but her heart was involved, and that hurt. She loved him, and she had told him so, once . . . perhaps several times before their marriage, but instead of returning her love he had taken it and used it to his own advantage. That was what she found so difficult to accept—and forgive.

She put her book down on the bedside table and switched off the light. She could hear Jarvis in the shower as she slid between the sheets, and she closed her eyes, determined to go to sleep, but sleep did not come easily to her that night. She could imagine Jarvis in the shower, the drops of water clinging to his tanned, virile body, and deep inside her there was an ache for which she despised herself intensely.

Oh, God! she groaned inwardly. What kind of woman have I become?

Jarvis emerged from the bathroom, but Gina did not stir. Let him think she was asleep, let him think anything, but don't let him come near her. Not now! Not now when she knew his touch would inflame her and shame her!

The bedroom door was opened and closed quietly. She heard his footsteps going down the passage, and the tension eased slowly from her taut body. She was safe, safe for this one night at least, and perhaps now she would sleep.

It was, however, quite futile trying to go to sleep after that argument with Jarvis. She tossed and turned restlessly in the darkness and she was still awake when he entered their bedroom two hours later. She felt the bed sag beneath his weight when he got in beside her, and she lay rigid, scarcely daring to breathe, but in that uncanny way of his he knew that she was still awake.

'Dammit, Gina, don't pretend to be asleep when you're not!' he accused, switching on the bedside light and lifting himself up on one elbow to look at her.

'I wasn't pretending,' she protested, turning her expressive face away from that glaring light which would reveal her statement as a lie, but his strong fingers gripped her chin and forced her to look at him.

'We've got to talk, Gina.'

He looked tired, she thought for the second time that night. The lines about his eyes and mouth seemed more pronounced, and she wanted to smooth them out with her fingers, but she dared not. 'Can't this discussion wait until morning?' she sighed.

'No, it can't.' He released her chin to brush a strand of red-gold hair away from her cheek, and his fingers lingered against her skin in a casual caress. 'I want you to know that I don't find marriage to you quite as intolerable as I may have made it sound earlier this evening.'

Gina stared up at him warily, and failed in her attempt to discover what lay behind those steel-grey eyes. 'Am I supposed to take that as a compliment?'

'You may take it whichever way you please, but I want us to stop hurting each other unnecessarily.' His

hand played with a heavy strand of her hair as if he
loved the silky texture of it between his fingers. 'I had
no legal control over that clause in my mother's will,
and I acknowledge the fact that you didn't deserve to
be tricked into this marriage, but, circumstances being
what they are, I do think we should make the best of
it.'

'You mean a year isn't exactly a lifetime, is it?' Her
mouth curved with a hint of that bitterness which had
been gnawing away at her since their wedding day.
'Two months have already passed quite swiftly, and
the remaining ten months might not be such an ordeal
if we decide to be nice to each other. Is that what
you're saying?'

'You could say so, yes.'

She searched his face for some sign of mockery, but
found none, and she dared to consider his suggestion.
The desire to create a harmonious atmosphere between
Jarvis and herself was something she had been
contemplating for some time, but his cynicism, his
mockery, and, to a large extent, his deceitful behaviour
before their marriage, had prevented her from making
the attempt. Should she agree to make the attempt
now? Love, after all, kindles love, and perhaps . . . !

'Oh, God!' she groaned, tears filling her eyes as that
forlorn hope manifested itself in her heart. Should she
take the chance?

'Gina?' he questioned her, moving closer to her
beneath the sheets until she could feel the disturbing
warmth of his body through the thinness of her
nightdress. 'Do we call a truce?'

'Yes,' she heard herself agreeing in a whisper, and
a hint of devilment lurked in his eyes as his fingers
trailed a fiery path to the base of her throat where
that treacherous pulse was throbbing erratically.

'Shall we seal our truce with a kiss?'

'Yes,' she whispered again, not caring at that moment if he should mock her eagerness, and she drew his head down to hers until his warm mouth claimed hers in a sensually arousing kiss that inflamed her with a need for more. 'I think we're going to seal our truce with more than a kiss,' she murmured without resentment against his mouth.

'You're damn right we are,' Jarvis laughed throatily, his hand dipping beneath the bodice of her filmy nightgown, and she trembled in response when his fingers stole around her softly rounded breast.

They made love fiercely and passionately, but there was a part of her that still remained untouched when they lay exhausted and physically sated in each other's arms. Gina hungered for that love which she knew he could never give her, but she would have to learn to live without it and, for the first time in all the weeks of their marriage, she went to sleep in Jarvis's arms.

CHAPTER SEVEN

VITTOROIO'S was filled almost to capacity on Friday
evening, but the Italian restaurateur and his staff
always succeeded in creating a tranquil atmosphere in
which to dine. Gina would, however, have preferred
to spend a quiet evening at home, but Jarvis had
insisted they celebrate their newly formed truce in
style, and Vittorio had been asked to bring out a
bottle of his best champagne. Their usual table in the
alcove was secluded, shielding them partially from the
rest of the patrons, and Gina had begun to relax and
enjoy her self when she caught a glimpse of Lilian
Ulrich dining with a fair-haired man at a table across
the restaurant.

Her heart plummeted. Had Jarvis known that Lilian
would be dining at Vittorio's on that particular
evening? Her mind was in a chaotic and somewhat
frantic mood until she took a firm hold on her thoughts
and told herself not to be silly. The fact that they were
dining at Vittorio's on the same night was a coincidence; a very unfortunate coincidence; but that was
all.

Gina tried to ignore the presence of the woman
who had, until a few months ago, featured so promi-
nently in Jarvis's life, but she found she was observing
Jarvis closely in an attempt to ascertain whether he
was aware of Lilian's presence. Not once did she catch
him glancing in that direction, but she could not, of
course, be sure.

During the course of their meal she looked up from
her beef Straganoff to find her glance colliding with

Jarvis'. There was an expression in his eyes that made
her pulse rate quicken as he reached across the table
to cover her hand with his.

'Have I told you yet this evening that you look
beautiful?' His eyes caressed her as he spoke, his
glance trailing from the silky radiance of her red-gold
hair down to where the low V of her evening gown
exposed the tantalising cleavage between her breasts,
and her nipples hardened unashamedly for his inspection against the clinging folds of the amber-coloured
material. 'When I look at you I find I can barely wait
for us to return to Eldorado where I'll have you to
myself,' he added with a lazy smile.

Her body tingled beneath the sensual warmth of his
glance. It had never ceased to astound her that she
reacted to him like this, but it no longer embarrassed
her that he could arouse her without actually touching
her.

'Neither can I wait,' she smiled provocatively, and
the flash of desire in his eyes was sufficient reward,
but his fingers tightened punishingly about her before
he released her hand.

'You choose the damedest places for confessions of
an arousing nature,' he rebuked her with a deep-
throated growl.

'So do you.'

'Touché,' he acknowledged, his strong features
relaxing in a rueful smile that made him look years
younger. 'You haven't been home for some weeks.
Shall we drive out to the farm early tomorrow morning
and stay until Sunday?'

'I'd prefer to spend this weekend alone with you at
Eldorado.'

'I think I like the sound of that,' he agreed, and the
warmth in his eyes made the blood flow a little faster
through her veins.

'Jarvis darling, how marvellous to see you here this evening!' Lilian Ulrich's musical and faintly accented voice intruded on their private world, and Gina raised her glance sharply to see the blonde pull up a chair to seat herself at their table without being invited. 'We meet again,' she remarked to Gina, her eyes cold despite the smile that curved her beautiful mouth.

'You've met Gina before?'

'Yes, darling,' Lilian answered Jarvis's surprised query.

'Didn't she tell you we met on your wedding day at Eldorado, and that I took the liberty of warning her that she might find you're a taker in some instances and not a giver?'

'It must have slipped her mind, but I dare say Gina would have gathered that information for herself,' Jarvis remarked drily, and a coldness trickled along Gina's spine when his shuttered glance met her's briefly across the table.

Won't you join us at our table for the remainder of the evening?' Lilian invited, placing a possessive hand on Jarvis's arm.

'We have no desire to join you at your table.' Jarvis declined Lilian's invitation bluntly and quite ruthlessly while he removed his arm from beneath her hand. 'You may not have noticed, but you're gatecrashing on a private party.'

Lilian drew a sharp, audible breath, but she recovered her composure with an admirable swiftness. 'You can be so brutally frank at times, my darling, but I'll forgive you as I always do, and I hope you'll save a dance for me later.'

She rose gracefully, her crimson evening gown shimmering and clinging to her seductively proportioned body as she returned to her table across the restaurant, and male heads turned to observe her progress, but Jarvis picked up his knife and fork and and continued eating as if nothing of significance had occured to interrupt their meal.

Gina should have rejoiced at the way he had dealt with Lilian, but instead she lost her appetite. She popped a morsel of food into her mouth, but lack of enthusiam seemed to change the superbly prepared Stroganoff into tasteless leather. If Jarvis had been aware of the fact that she was merely toying with her food, then he did not comment on it, and her plate was removed some time later, the food practically untouched.

The band was playing a slow, romantic Gershwin tune when Jarvis led Gina on to the floor. He held her close, their bodies touching when they danced, but the magic of the moment was marred by the disquieting thoughts racing through her mind. She had been used as leverage by her godmother to disrupt the relationship between Jarvis and Lilian, and she did need a psychoanalyst to explain to her that attraction between two people could be enhanced by the mere fact that they had been forced to terminate their relationship prematurely.

Lilian's violet-blue eyes were observing them from across the restaurant, and the message in those eyes seemed to confirm Gina's suspicions: You've poached on my terrain, and I don't like it!

'Relax, Gina,' Jarvis ordered, his arm tightening possessively about her taut body. 'And stop behaving as if I'm not here.'

'I was thinking,' she apologised hastily. 'You were rather nasty to Lilian . . . quite rude, in fact.'

'That's the only language she understands.' The knife-edge coldness in his voice sent an involuntary shiver racing through her. 'You have no reason to feel uncomfortable.'

Gina's head shot up to encounter the gleam of mockery in his steel-grey eyes, and she expelled the

air from her lungs on a shaky laugh. 'You read me so
well that it scares me sometimes,' she confessed.

'You have nothing to fear from Lilian.'

'I wonder, Gina thought cynically while she made a
concerted effort to ignore the fact that Lilian's eyes
had never left them for an instant while they danced.

They talked and flirted mildly with each other when
they returned to their table to drink their coffee, but
Gina did not quite succeed in shaking off the
disquieting feeling that Lilian Ulrich had no intention
of allowing the evening to pass without making her
displeasure known.

Gina left the table later and her suspicions were
confirmed when she closed the padded door to the
ladies' room behind her to find that she was not alone.
Lilian was there, and she was taking her time with the
reparations to her make-up as if she had waited for
this moment. Their eyes met in the mirror, and Gina
was aware of icy shivers racing along her spine when
Lilian snapped the cap on to her lipstick and turned
to face her with a smile.

'What did you use as bait to lure Jarvis into
marriage?' she asked bluntly, studying Gina with a
speculative and vindictive gleam in her eyes. 'Did you
withhold yourself from him sexually?'

'I consider your question impertinent!' snapped
Gina, her body stiffening with indignation and anger.

'Perhaps so,' Lilian agreed. 'Jarvis has a way with
women, and he always gets what he wants. If you
were not withholding yourself from him sexually, then
I can only assume once again that he stood to gain
something of importance by marrying you, and I
suspect you've discovered what it is.'

'I know why Jarvis married me,' Gina answered her
with a calmness she was far from experiencing, 'and
the reason why he chose to do so doesn't concern
you.'

'It does concern me,' Lilian contradicted her with a venomous smile curving her mouth. 'Jarvis and I belong together, and this cruel intervention on our happiness is a matter I will not overlook. I shall make it my business to discover the truth, and I will not leave one stone unturned until I do.'

Lilian walked out of the ladies' room, but her heady perfume hovered in the air like a lingering threat. *You have nothing to fear from Lilian,* Jarvis had said, but Gina was not in agreement with him. Lilian Ulrich was a calculating and determined woman who would not rest until she had uncovered the truth, and Gina also knew that this woman would not hesitate to subject her to a brand of humiliation that would finally crucify her.

Gina remained in the ladies' room until she had controlled her nervous tremors sufficiently to go out and face Jarvis. She dabbed powder on her nose and added a touch of colour to her lips, but there was little she could do to improve the sickly pallor of her cheeks. Nothing ever escaped Jarvis's notice, and she could only hope that her paleness would go unnoticed in the dimly-lit restaurant.

Lilian was nowhere in sight when Gina made her way hesitantly among the tables to where Jarvis was waiting for her. He rose at once to pull out her chair, and she smiled up at him in a way she hoped would look natural, but his glance sharpened on her features and his mouth tightened.

'You're very pale, Gina.' His hand gripped her arm before she could sit down. 'Aren't you feeling well?'

His keen perception shattered her fragile hopes that her appearance would go unnoticed, and his unexpected gentleness and concern brought her horribly close to bursting into tears, but she somehow managed to control herself.

'I—I think I must have eaten something that—that didn't agree with me.' She said the first thing that came to mind, but she could not look at him while she spoke. 'It will pass, I'm sure.'

Jarvis seemed to hestiate a moment before he said abruptly, 'I'm taking you home.'

He did not attempt to make conversation during the drive back to Eldorado, and Gina was intensely grateful for his silence. Her throat felf as if someone had taken a stranglehold on it, and her jaw was so firmly clenched with tension and unhappiness that she could not speak even if she had wanted to. She had foolishly credited Lilian with a victory by allowing her to mar an evening which had started out as a celebration dinner, but Gina could not alter the way she felt. She was afraid: afraid of the power that woman might still wield where Jarvis was concerned, and afraid of the harm it could do to a marriage which had been perpetrated for all the wrong reasons.

'Do you have something to take, or would you like me to go out and get you a medication from the all-night emergency chemist?' Jarvis questioned her when they entered their bedroom at Eldorado, and Gina stared at him blankly for a moment before she realised what he was referring to.

'I have something,' she lied, taking two headache tablets out of the dressing-table drawer and swallowing them with a glass of water in the bathroom.

She cursed herself later. She had behaved like a frightened child. She felt guilty, and she had to make it up to Jarvis somehow.

'Are you feeling better?' he asked when she lowered herself on to the bed beside him.

'Much better.' Her green gaze was apologetic when it met his. 'I'm sorry if I spoiled the evening for us.'

'The evening isn't over yet,' he smiled, a fire smouldering in his eyes as he sat up in bed to lift the lacy

straps of her nightgown off her smooth shoulders. The
flimsy garment slithered down to leave her naked from
the waist up. 'The evening has only just begun for us,'
he added throatily.

'I'm so glad,' she agreed, her voice no more than a
distracted whisper when his fingers gently stroked her
taut, pointed breasts.

The rush of blood into her nipples was achingly
sweet, and her gasp of pleasure was smothered against
his mouth when he pulled her down on to the bed
beside him with one arm locked about her waist while
his free hand stripped off her nightdress. She wanted
him so much that she met fire with fire until she was
immersed in an inferno that robbed her of everything
except the need to give as much as she was receiving.

'You're so beautiful I want to kiss you all over,'
Jarvis groaned, and Gina felt no alarm, only an
intense and erotic pleasure when his hot, seeking
mouth began its slow and meticulous exploration of
her body until every pulse was throbbingly alive to his
touch.

'I want you, Jarvis! I want you *now*!' she begged,
her body moving beneath his with a wild and primitive
urgency which was alien to her. '*Please*! Please take
me!'

'Not yet, my sweet,' he murmured against her
smooth, pulsating throat, his hands stroking her
passionately eager body and stilling her in much the
same manner that she used to stem the quivering
impatience of her Arab stallion. 'We have the entire
night, and I'm going to make sure we enjoy every
minute of it.'

Gina was too drugged with desire to wonder if he
was joking, but she would soon have discovered that
he was not. His lovemaking that night was a prolonged
and achingly sweet torment that made her fear at
times that she might die with the pleasure of it. Jarvis

was in complete control, and she submitted to the
dominance of his powerful, thrusting body by allowing
him to take her where he pleased until a shuddering
cry of exaltation escaped her as the world seemed to
explode around her and leave her trembling and
trapped in the wake of its ferocity.

It was much later, when Jarvis lay sleeping beside
her, that Gina's thoughts turned again to Lilian. *Jarvis
and I belong together,* Lilian had said, *and this cruel
intervention on our happiness is a matter I will not
overlook.*

Gina did not want to hazard a guess as to Jarvis's
feelings, but her own were perfectly clear. She loved
him, and she hoped and prayed that as the year
progressed he might learn to care for her in return.
She knew that he found her attractive and desirable,
but that meant nothing at all. He was capable of
finding any number of women attractive and desirable,
but she happened to be there for him. She was the
woman he had been forced to make his wife, and
there was no sense in deluding herself that she meant
anything more to him at the moment than a means to
an end. Eldorado was the prize, and Evelyn Cain had
been correct in saying that Jarvis would do anything
to get it.

Gina would not have believed that a foolish and
unfortunate accident could disrupt the harmonious
atmosphere at Eldorado within a few short weeks, but
it did. She had planned a special dinner party at
Eldorado as a surprise for Jarvis to celebrate his
thirty-sixth birthday, and she had invited a few of his
closest friends to join them that evening.

She was in an excited and slightly distracted mood
when she hurried downstairs that afternoon to make
sure that her instructions to the kitchen staff were
being carried out, and as she flew down the last flight

of stairs the heel of her shoe caught in a loose thread in the carpet. For one terrifying, heart-stopping instant Gina was still upright, and then the world took on a new, sickening dimension as she rolled and bumped down the remaining steps into the hall below.

A scream echoed through the silent house. It could only have come from her, but she could not recall a sound passing her lips during that painful, tumbling passage down the stairs. She lay stunned for a fraction of a second, her eyes wide and questioning as she looked up at the circle of anxious faces which had appeared above her, and then an excruciating pain tore at her savagely and unexpectedly. A cry of agony rose in her throat, but she slipped into that mercifully dark abyss of unconsciousness before a sound escaped her.

Gina came to her senses a few hours later to find herself lying flat on her back in a strange bed with a strange man and a white-clad woman hovering over her.

'Who are you, and where am I?' she questioned them in a voice which she could not raise above a painful whisper.

'I'm Dr Hirshfield, and you're in hospital, Mrs Cain,' the man with the dark-rimmed spectacles answered her, a suggestion of a smile lifting the corners of his mouth. 'You had a nasty accident, do you remember?'

An accident? Gina stared blankly at the high ceiling, and then something clicked in her brain. She nodded in reply to the doctor's query, and a look of relief flashed across the faces of the two people who had been observing her so intently.

'Falling down those stairs was such a damn silly thing to do,' she added, trying to laugh away her embarrassment, but the effort seemed to exhaust her and stab painfully at her ribs.

'You're a very lucky woman,' Dr Hirshfield explained gravely. 'We're treating you for bruises and possible concussion, but I'm afraid there was nothing we could do to save the child you were carrying.'

Gina's face went a shade paler against the stark white linen on that hospital bed, and for one terrible moment it felt as if her head was going to crack wide open. A child! She had been carrying Jarvis's child! Dear God, was that possible?

'How . . . I mean, why . . . ' Her bewildered voice croaked into silence, and Dr Hirshfield did not quite succeed in disguising his surprise and concern.

'I gather you didn't know you were pregnant?'

Gina shook her head mutely, her eyes filling with tears she could not suppress, and she swallowed with difficulty to rid herself of that painful lump in her throat before she risked using her voice to ask, 'How—how far was I?'

'I would say you'd been six to seven weeks into pregnancy,' the doctor explained quietly. 'I would, however, like to assure you that there was no internal damage, and there's nothing to prevent you from having other children.'

Gina's mind was spinning like a rocket which had veered off its plotted course, and it required several agonising seconds of deep concentration before she was capable of thinking rationally. The anxiety to maintain that new, harmonious level in her relationship with Jarvis had caused her to overlook the irregularity in her normal body functions, and then there had also been that slight stab of nausea which had plagued her on a few occasions at the breakfast table during the past weeks. The signs of pregnancy had been glaringly obvious, but she had foolishly ignored them. Oh, God, how had it happened? How and when could they have been so careless? To bring a child into their marriage would have been a disaster, but . . . oh, God, to lose it was something she would mourn for the rest of her life!

'Does my husband know?' she questioned the doctor nervously, and that rugged, bespectacled face above her nodded gravely.

'I told him the moment we brought you out of the theatre.'

'What—what did he say?' she croaked, making a feeble attempt to wipe her tears away with her fingers until the nurse completed the mopping up process with a paper hankerchief.

'He never said anything, but he looked as stunned as most husbands do when confronted with the news I had to give him.' Dr Hirshfield smiled reassuringly, but he would never guess at the fear which was lacing itself through her chaotic emotions at that moment. 'Your husband is waiting to see you, but I'll send him only if you promise not to tire yourself,' the doctor's pleasant voice intruded on her thoughts. 'You need rest, and plenty of it, at the moment.'

The doctor gestured authoritatively to the nurse, and Gina was left alone in that private ward for a few minutes to take stock of herself. She was aching all over, but there was an ache deep inside her which she knew could have nothing to do with the superficial bruises she had sustained. She had been mentally crippled by the simultaneous discovery that she had been pregnant and had miscarried, but, as the shock wore off, she became aware of new feelings churning through her which she had neither the strength nor the courage to analyse at that moment.

'Gina?'

Jarvis seemed to materialise from out of nowhere beside her hospital bed, and she swallowed convulsively to rid herself of the tears which treatened to choke her once again.

'I'm sorry,' she whispered, forcing her unsteady lips into a smile as she looked up into his grim, ashen face. 'This wasn't part of the surprise I'd planned for your birthday, and——' She broke off in a panic as her mind registered the preparations which had gone into her desire to make that evening a success. 'Oh, Lord, what are we going to do about all those people I invited?'

'Rosie found your guest list, and she called everyone to cancel the arrangements.' Steel-grey eyes held hers compellingly while his hand found hers on the white coverlet, and his grip on her fingers was so fierce that she almost cried out with the agony of it. 'Why didn't you tell me you were pregnant?'

'I didn't know.' Her eyes misted with the tears which seemed to come so easily in her weakened state. 'I honestly didn't know.'

The bruising pressure of his fingers lessened, and an angry, ragged sigh escaped him. 'My God, you're lucky you didn't kill yourself today.'

Was there an accusation in his voice, or was she imagining it? Was he annoyed that, despite their precautions, she had succeeded in getting herself pregnant, or was he annoyed that she had lost the baby? The latter seemed improbable, but she was physically and mentally too weak to decide, and neither could she control a wave of cynical depression that was beginning to engulf her.

'It would have been luckier still for you if I *had* succeeded in killing myself. My death would have set you free.'

She could not explain what had prompted her to say that, she certainly had not intended to, but it was too late to retract that terrible statement and the damage it had done. Jarvis had gone white about the mouth, and his features had settled into a granite-hard, impenetrable mask that filled her with a sense of foreboding.

'You need to get some rest,' he announced in a clipped and impersonal voice that chilled her. 'I'll see you again tomorrow.'

The tears spilled freely down her cheeks from the moment he left, and she was still crying weakly when the nurse walked into her room some minutes later. It was reaction, the nurse explained, jabbing a needle into Gina's arm, and the tears finally subsided as a blessed drowsiness invaded her mind.

Gina could not decide whether she felt better or worse the following day. She was so stiff and sore that she could barely move, and her head was pounding as if someone was knocking a hammer against her skull.

Jarvis came again that evening to see her, but his visit was brief and his polite, impersonal questions left her weeping once again with the desparing knowledge that she had only herself to blame for the cool, distant stranger he had become.

Gina was allowed to go home on the morning of the second day after the accident. Jarvis collected her at the hospital that Saturday morning, and drove her back to Eldorado where he escorted her safely up to their bedroom.

'I'm sending Rosie up to help you pack a suitcase,' he said in the clipped voice she had learned to dislike intensely. 'I'm taking you out to the farm after lunch. The change of scenery will be good for you, and I'll fetch you again in two weeks' time.'

'I'd rather stay here,' she protested, afraid of what this separation might do to their swiftly crumbling relationship, and she was so desperately in need of an opportunity to make amends for the dreadful remark she had made that first night in hospital.

'It's all arranged, Georgina.' His jaw was set in a hard, unrelenting line as he brushed aside her protest in a court manner. 'I have a difficult murder trial coming up, and I'm going to be working almost day and night during the next two weeks. The farm is the best place for you in the circumstances, and your father agrees with me on this issue.'

He turned on his heel and strode out of the room, and she was left with a numb acceptance of something she did not have the strength to alter. He was taking her home to her family for two weeks, and that seemed to be that.

Gina had to admit during those fourteen days on the farm that she would have been of little or no use to Jarvis if she had remained at Eldorado. She would, in fact, have achieved nothing by remaining there. She had suffered severe bouts of deep depression and moments when that deep sense of loss would make her weep herself into a state of exhaustion, but her family had rallied round to comfort her and boost her moral in their own quiet way. Her pregnancy and subsequent miscarriage were never mentioned, but Gina could not forget it. She had lost something precious, something she could never reclaim, and she had to resign herself to the certain knowledge that her mental bruises would take considerably longer to heal than the physical ones she had sustained in that disastrous tumble down Eldorado's stairs.

To have Jarvis's children had been something she had dreamed of before their marriage, but Aunt Evelyn's will had cruelly killed that dream in its infancy. She had known on their wedding day that having a baby would have to be deleted from the agenda of her marriage to Jarvis. A child would merely aggravate the delicate and sometimes explosive situation, but she could not help wishing she had not had that stupid accident. There would be other children, the doctor had said, but that was not quite true. If she could not have Jarvis's children then she would prefer not to have any at all. No other man could ever take Jarvis's place, and that was something she had to accept and learn to live with.

The period of truce was over, Gina realised when she returned to Eldorado, and it was not the fact that the stairs had been recarpeted that had alerted her to this new development in her unconventional marriage. It was the shattering discovery that Jarvis had moved out of the master bedroom during her absence and into the room across the passage that had given her an insight into what the future held in store for her, and it hurt. It hurt her more than she had imagined possible, and the explanation for this drastic transition was painfully and glaringly obvious. He was afraid she might become pregnant again, and a child would merely strengthen the chains which held him in unwilling bondage.

The routine at Eldorado might not always have been stable, but it was completely disrupted during the weeks that followed. Gina not only had to accustom herself to the loneliness of her nights in the four-poster bed, she was also confronted with the frightening knowledge that there was an almost complete break in communication between Jarvis and herself, and she was nearly frantic in the face of her inability to do something constructive about it.

Their new existence did not seem to cause Jarvis the slightest discomfort. He frequently came home late at night, and the calls from his secretary, telling Gina not to expect him home for dinner, had become a regular and embarrassing occurrence. He was going through an unusually busy period, he had explained once when Gina had summoned up sufficient courage to question him, and she had no cause to disbelieve him until the day she had found traces of lipstick on a handkerchief which she had removed from the pocket of a suit prior to sending it to the cleaners. The lipstick was a deep crimson, the colour Lilian Ulrich favoured. That was not sufficient proof on which to base an accusation, but it placed Gina on the alert to something she prayed could not be true.

Jarvis displayed characteristics quite alien to his nature on the few evenings when he favoured Gina with his presence at Eldorado's dinner table. He would be morose and irritable, and their meal would invariably end in an argument after which he would storm out of the house, or closet himself in the study until the early hours of the morning.

Gina was completely at a loss. She felt as if she had been caught in a vicious, punishing trap from which there was no escape, and she decided finally that the only way to deal with the pain would be to steal herself mentally against future attacks.

She had, at length, considered herself prepared for anything, but she was caught off guard one morning when she opened Eldorado's front door to find Lilian Ulrich standing on the doorstep.

'May I come in?' Lilian asked, and Gina gestured her inside in silence while she took the time to gather her scattered wits about her. Lilian stepped into the hall, her expensive perfume filling the air as she cast a critical glance about her. 'This really is a lovely old house, but rather antiquated, don't you think?'

Gina could almost feel her godmother's bristling displeasure enfolding her as if it were her own. Eldorado was an old, but a well-preserved house, and each room had been furnished to give it an individual character. Gina loved this old house as it stood, and to modernise it would be tantamount to defiling a consecrated monument to the past.

'I presume you're of the opinion that Eldorado needs to be redecorated in a more contemporary style?' Gina commented distastefully on Lilian's remark

as she directed her unexpected and unwanted guest
into the living-room.

'I most certainly am of that opinion,' Lilian
admitted, her cold, calculating glance sweeping the
room from its high, beamed ceiling down to the
priceless Persian rugs on the floor. 'And I shall take a
personal delight in doing so as soon as your foolish
marriage has ended,' she added with venomous relish
as she lowered herself gracefully on to an Elizabethan
chair.

Stay calm, Gina warned herself, but she felt quiver-
ingly taut as she seated herself in the high-backed
chair Evelyn Cain had favoured, oddly drawing
comfort and strength from it.

'You sound very sure of yourself,' she said coldly.

'Oh, but I am,' Lilian smiled, but her attractive,
violet-blue eyes remained cold and assessing. 'I know
a disillusioned and discontented woman when I see
one.'

Lilian was clever, and she was quick too, but Gina's
face gave nothing away in her desperate fight not to
allow her adversary an easy victory. 'You're mistaken.
Jarvis and I are perfectly happy together.'

'Darling, I hate to contradict you, but I happen to
know him so much better than you do.' Lilian crossed
one expensively stockinged leg over the other, and her
perfectly arched brows were raised above cold,
mocking eyes. 'Jarvis hasn't been himself lately. The
bonds of marriage are beginning to chafe uncomfortably, and very soon now he'll want his freedom. I can
read the signs so well. You see, Jarvis and I are two
of a kind, and I could have told you on your wedding
day that you don't have what it takes to hold a man
like Jarvis Cain. It's me he wants, my dear, and it's
to me he escapes periodically, since I've placed no
bars on the cage of our relationship, so don't be
surprised if one day soon he spreads his wings and

leaves your cage permanently.'

Her confidence and calm conceit succeeded in leaving Gina speechless and strangely numb when Lilian rose elegantly to her feet and opened her handbag to take out a grey and blue striped tie which looked vaguely familiar to Gina.

'The reason I came here this morning was to return this,' she said, a self-satisfied and slightly triumphant smile on her lips as she carefully draped the tie over the back of the chair she had vacated. 'Jarvis left it at my place the other night, and I happen to know it's a favourite of his.'

Gina silently blessed that icy numbness inside her. It gave her the strength to escort Lilian off the premises without making a fool of herself, and an eternity seemed to elapse before the numbness eased away, to be replaced by a leaden pain. It settled suffocatingly in her chest seemingly determined to remain there.

She collected the tie Lilian had left in the living-room, and in her anguished state of mind her fingers tightened about the silky material until her knuckles whitened. Her suspicions had been confirmed. Jarvis was spending his free time with Lilian, but Lilian was still unaware of the fact that Jarvis would not discard the shackles of this unwanted marriage until he could rightfully claim Eldorado as his own.

Dear God! How can he do this to me? What did I do to deserve this humiliation? It is because I dared to love him that he is so intent on destroying me?

What are you going to do about it? The question leapt into her tortured mind and she could find no answer to it. She wanted to leave Jarvis, she wanted to end this marriage which had become a painful imprisonment, but for Jarvis's sake, and Eldorado's, she could not do it.

Jarvis arrived home early that evening for the first time in days, but he barely spoke to her before he went upstairs to shower and change, and later, when they sat down to dinner, Gina made no attempt at conversation. Jarvis was too engrossed in his own thoughts to notice anything amiss, and her mind was filled with the unpleasant memory of what had occurred that morning. His tie lay on her dressing-table where she had left it, but she was still hurting too much to confront him sensibly with the evidence of his infidelity which Lilian had so thoughtfully provided.

You don't have what it takes to hold a man like Jarvis Cain. Lilian's words had been viciously barbed, and they still had the power to inflict a cruel, agonising wound.

Gina studied Jarvis unobtrusively while she toyed with her dessert that evening. He projected an aggressively masculine image which never failed to attract women. He possessed a quality of steely strength which was tempered with an underlying but distinct aura of controlled sensuality, and Gina had not been unaware of the way single and married women alike had stared at him at the many public functions she had attended with him. His lean body had the ability to move with the lithe agility and toned muscles of a primed athlete, and his piercing, analytical grey eyes could disorientate and excite rather than repel a woman.

If there were women who had spent time fantasising about him, then Gina could not blame them. Her own fantasies had died a cruel death on their wedding day. She had dreamed of loving and being loved, and of making Eldorado a home again for the man she loved, but it had been nothing but a fantasy. The reality was cold and harsh, and the fire of her dreams had turned to ashes.

Lilian had known what she was talking about, Gina admitted the galling truth to herself. She did not have the ability to hold a man like Jarvis. Their marriage had been a necessity forced on him by the conditions laid down in his mother's will and, after four months of living together, his interest in her as a woman had waned with considerable help from the new fear that a child might be born into this marriage he had not wanted. What was it Lilian had said? *Jarvis hasn't been himself lately. The bonds of marriage are beginning to chafe uncomforatably.*

'I'll have my coffee in the study.' Jarvis jolted her back to the present, and she looked up sharply when he rose from the dinner table. 'I have an important case lined up for tomorrow,' he explained.

Had there been a glimmer of an apology in his grey, hooded eyes, or had she imagined it?

'I'll ask Rosie to prepare some coffee for you.'

He nodded and turned away, leaving her with the despairing conviction that she was a glutton for punishment. Jarvis did not love her, he never would, and yet she went on searching and hoping for some small sign that he cared.

O, what a tanlged web we weave when first we practise to deceive, a half-forgotten question came to mind. Jarvis had been the first to practise deception, and now she was trying to deceive herself by reaching for something that had as little substance as a shadow.

CHAPTER EIGHT

GINA got out of bed with difficulty the following morning. The long, wakeful hours during the night had been filled with painful, humiliating and despairing thoughts, and had culminated in a slow, simmering anger which had lit a smouldering fire in her green eyes.

She was leaving her room to go down to the breakfast-room when she found herself confronted by Jarvis in the passage outside her door. He was wearing a dark blue suit which accentuated his good looks, and his white shirt was open at the throat.

'If you're looking for your grey and blue striped tie, it's lying on the dressing-table,' she forestalled his query instinctively as she brushed past him, and was gratifyingly aware of the surprised look in his eyes before she turned and walked down the passage.

'How did you know I was looking for my tie, and what's it doing on your dressing-table?'

'You are in some ways a creature of habit,' she said coldly, pausing on the top landing to face him. 'You never leave your bedroom unless you're fully dressed for whatever the occasion, so it was natural for me to assume that you were looking for your tie.'

'That doesn't explain why my tie is lying on your dressing-table,' he reminded her curtly, his eyes narrowed and speculative, and Gina lifted her shoulders slightly in a carefully contrived gesture of indifference.

'Lilian delivered it personally yesterday morning,' she explained, her voice calm and controlled despite

that fierce desire inside her to strike out savagely in
retaliation to the pain he was inflicting on her. 'You
apparently left it at her place the other night.'

She turned to go down the carpeted stairs, but
Jarvis was beside her in an instant, his fingers biting
cruelly through the woollen sleeve of her dress into
the soft flesh of her upper arm.

'You may not realise it, but you've made a veiled
accusation which I consider needs clarification.'

She stared down at those lean, strong fingers which
could arouse her so skilfully, and the pain of despair
deep inside her brought tears to her eyes which she
blinked away hastily for fear that he might notice
them and mock her.

'I was stating a fact rather than making an accusation, and there's no need for a clarification.' She bit
out the words, not daring to look at him until she was
convinced she had controlled herself sufficiently.

A muttered oath escaped him when she attempted
to free her arm from those punishing fingers, and his
mouth was set in a tight, angry line when he marched
her unceremoniously down the passage and into the
bedroom they no longer shared. He closed the door
firmly behind them, and there was a nervous edge to
the angry beat of her heart when he turned to face
her.

'If you consider clarification unnecessary, then I
imagine it must be an explanation you want of me,'
he mocked her, and she turned on him in a fury before
he could continue.

'I would prefer it if you didn't insult my intelligence
by trying to explain away the fact that you've resumed
your long-standing relationship with Lilian Ulrich.'
Her voice was icy with bitterness and distaste, and the
angry fire was clearly visible in her green, shadowed
eyes when they met his. 'I have an intense dislike for
Lilian and women of her kind. She is, as your mother

once said, a hard-faced woman whose only interest in
you is for material gain, but if you're too blind to see
it, then that's your business entirely. I must, however,
credit her with honesty. She made no secret of the fact
that you were seeing each other again, and that you
would continue to see each other, but there's one
small fact which she doesn't have in her possession.
She doesn't know that your passion for her is pale
beside your passion for Eldorado, but in the end she'll
discover the truth in the same painful and humiliating
way I did.' She drew a shuddering breath and fought
to control herself before she continued. 'I pity her,
Jarvis, but I pity you most of all. You don't know
what love is, and you will never know the lasting joy
of giving, only the brief pleasure of taking. Lilian was
right when she said you are two of a kind. You belong
together, but you'll both have to wait, since I don't
intend to stand accused of robbing you of your home.'

There had been a telltale break in her husky voice
before it faded into the tense, explosive silence which
prevailed, and an odd chill of fear raced up her spine
when she saw Jarvis's features settle into a mask of
fury which she had never encountered before.

'Have you quite finished?' he demanded in a quiet,
clipped voice, and a nerve was jumping ominously in
his cheek while he clenched and unclenched his hands
at his sides as if he were having difficulty in controlling
the desire to place them about her throat.

'Yes!' she snapped in a defiance born of fear. 'I've
said all I intend to say.'

'Well, let me tell you something, Georgina,' he
continued in that same dangerously quiet tone of voice
that chilled her to the marrow. 'Jealousy and suspicion
are the two qualities I despise most in a woman, and
you've just shown me that you possess both those
qualities. I may not know what love is, but I damn
well know when I can trust someone. Trust is a

tangible emotion. Try it some time if you have the stomach for it, and you may find it of some benefit to you, but until then I suggest you keep your suspicions and your jealousies to yourself!'

He turned on his heel and snatching up the offending tie, stalked out of the room, slamming the door behind him with such savagery that Gina flinched in fearful anticipation that the delicate panes might shatter in the shuddering window frames.

Trust! 'Try it some time if you have the stomach for it,' Jarvis had instructed. Dear God, he surely did not expect her to trust him in the face of all odds! She couldn't do that, could she?

The house seemed ominously silent that morning after Jarvis's stormy departure. He had left the house without having breakfast, and he had also left Gina with a great deal to think about. He had accused her of being jealous and suspicious, and she had to admit to herself that she had harboured both those despicable emotions. She could blame it on extenuating circumstances, and also on Lilian Ulrich's deliberate interference, but she knew that the solution lay within herself.

So what if Jarvis had married her for the sole purpose of inheriting Eldorado! Was she going to relinquish the battle without a fight? Was she going to let him go without making an attempt to win his affection, if not his love?

Gina's mind was reeling with positive and faintly aggressive thoughts, but it took hours of soul-searching that morning before she finally knew what she had to do. She entered Eldorado's magnificent hall and lifted the telephone receiver to dial Jarvis's number at the office before she changed her mind. She wanted to ask him to meet her somewhere for lunch, and this time, perhaps, they might be able to talk without striking out at each other verbally.

'Mr Cain's office, good morning.' His secretary answered almost instantly, and nervous anxiety made Gina's heart beat heavily against her ribs.

'Good morning, Mrs Jackson. I'd like to speak to my husband, please.'

'I'm afraid Mr Cain isn't in at the moment. He's having lunch with Mrs Ulrich, and I don't expect him back before three this afternoon. Could I ask him to give you a call the moment he returns to the office, Mrs Cain?'

'No.' Gina staggered mentally beneath the feeling that she had been dealt a savage blow to a most vulnerable area. 'That won't be necessary, thank you. Goodbye.'

She dropped the receiver on to its cradle and sat down heavily on the chair beside the rosewood table when her legs threatened to cave in beneath her. She was shaking, and she was hurting, and through the mist of pain that surrounded her came Jarvis's accusing voice.

Jealousy and suspicion are the two qualities I despise most in a woman. Trust is a tangible emotion. Try it some time if you have the stomach for it.

Jealousy and suspicion were running rampant in Gina's mind at that moment, and trust came a poor third. She was jealous of the time he was spending with Lilian, and she was suspicious of the reason for it. How could she trust him if he gave her no reason to do so? How could she have faith in a man who had employed the method he had used to trick her into marriage, and who she knew had every intention of casting her aside like a soiled shirt as soon as he had complied with the unfair stipulations in his mother's will?

Oh, God, please give me strength! she prayed silently when she got up and left the house to stroll aimlessly through the sunlit garden where the gardener was raking up the leaves which had fallen on the lawn.

Jarvis arrived home at ten that evening. Gina heard him go into his bedroom across the passage from her own, and some minutes later she heard him in the shower. She tried desperately to shut her mind to his presence in the house, but every nerve and sinew seemed to be on the alert. She tried to convince herself that she hated him, but her hatred melted away like ice in the summer sun when he entered her bedroom unexpectedly half an hour later.

Drops of moisture were still glistening on his dark hair, and she knew from experience that he never wore anything beneath the wine-red towelling robe that left his legs bare from the knees down. This intimate knowledge was having a disastrous effect on her senses, and from deep within the core of her womanhood there rose a trembling, aching need which she tried desperately to quell as he approached the bed and seated himself close enough for her to be aware of the clean, male smell of him. Oh, how she despised herself for being so weak! Did she have no pride? Jarvis had hurt her more than anyone else ever could, but her love for him had somehow survived to make her wonder how much more it would take before her feelings were completely crushed. It had been several weeks since the last time he had made love to her, but she had never felt the deprivation as strongly as she felt it at that moment. She wanted him to touch her, to hold her, and fill that aching void inside her until she was mindless with the ecstasy of their union.

'Mrs Jackson told me you called the office today while I was out.' His glance was piercingly intent, and it unnerved her. 'Was there something of importance you wanted to discuss with me?'

'Yes—no—oh, it was a spur-of-the-moment thing, really, and I——' Gina halted nervously and lowered her gaze to the magazine she was mutilating between her agitated fingers. 'I was hoping you'd be free for us to have lunch together somewhere in town so we could talk as we used to without all the antagonism and tension between us,' she confessed, choosing the truth in favour of subterfuge.

'It was a nice thought.'

'Yes, well . . . ' She drew a steadying breath and shrugged with an affected casualness. 'It never went beyond a thought since you were out to lunch with Lilian, and you weren't expected back before three.'

'We could talk now, if you want to?' he suggested, making no attempt at an explanation, and his calm, unperturbed manner ignited a spark of anger she had difficulty in controlling.

'The setting isn't right, and neither is the mood.'

'Are you saying we need to have a table between us to conduct a sensible conversation?' he mocked her.

'No,' she corrected, her need of him waning swiftly beneath that surging wave of bitterness. 'I'm saying that the moment is gone, and it can't be recaptured.'

'Just as this moment will never be recaputred if we let it pass.' Jarvis removed the sad-looking magazine from her hands and flung it on to the carpeted floor. 'What did you want to discuss with me, Gina?'

Dear heaven! His towelling robe was open almost to his waist, and even in this moment of disappointment and anger she had to fight against the desire to reach out and slide her hands across his powerful chest where the dark hair curled tightly against his tanned skin. He was much too close for comfort, she had to get away from him if she did not want to humiliate herself, and she slid out of bed, reaching for her silk dressing gown as her feet touched the carpeted floor.

'What I wanted to discuss with you is no longer relevant, but there's another matter which I've been giving a considerable amount of thought lately.' She did not look at him while she slipped her arms into the wide sleeves and tied the belt firmly about her waist. 'I'd like to work again, and there's a possibility that I may get my old job back.'

There was a brief, tense silence before he said, 'I thought we'd agreed that there was no necessity for you to work.'

'That was before our marriage.' There was a bitter anguish in the memory of dreams which had so carelessly been shattered, and she hastily veiled the pain in her eyes before she turned to face him. 'Jarvis, I'll go mad if I have to sit around and stagnate for much longer. You've employed adequate staff to take care of the house and the grounds, and they do it so well that I'm almost superfluous. My days are spent wandering aimlessly about the house, or going into the city to shop for something I don't really need, and my nights . . . ' Her throat tightened, and her hands fluttered in an unconscious gesture of despair. 'My nights are mostly spent dining alone and staring at walls which are beginning to crowd in on me.'

He rose abruptly, and his compelling glance held hers as he stepped round the foot of the bed to join her in front of the window. 'I'm lonely too, Gina.'

'Oh, don't make me laugh!' she snorted disparagingly. 'You have your work to keep you occupied, and you have Lilian to entertain you when you're free.'

'Dammit, do you have to bring Lilian into this?'

'Why not?' she questioned him cynically, her hand clutching at the back of the armchair for support when she found herself looking a long way up into his furious grey eyes. 'She's become as much a part of my life as she is of yours!'

'What kind of man do you think I am?' he demanded harshly. 'Do you credit me with so little decency that you could accuse me of having an affair with Lilian while I'm married to you?'

'I have only your actions in the past to use as a guide,' she responded coldly. 'If you were callous enough to use my feelings as leverage to trick me into marrying you, then you can't blame me for thinking you're capable of having an affair with Lilian while our marriage continues its distasteful course through to the end of the stipulated period.'

'For God's sake, Gina, you——'

We were discussing my intention to return to work,' she reminded him sharply, taking a hasty pace away from him to avoid the hand that reached out for her, and his heavy brows drew together in an angry frown.

'I don't want you to work again.'

'Why not?' she smiled up at him cynically. 'Does it give your ego a boost to know that I'm here, and that I might be available on those occasions when it's inconvenient for Lilian to have you in her bed?'

He went strangely white about the mouth. 'My God, Gina, you go too far!'

'Does the truth hurt?' she demanded, blind to all the danger signals while she tried desperately to cope with the agonising pain which was tearing at her soul like the savage talons of an eagle.

'*Your* idea of the truth hurts,' he countered harshly through his teeth, advancing towards her with an ominous expression on his lean, handsome face. 'I'm not entirely without feelings, and it may surprise you to know that I do have a conscience, but this is one night when I'm not going to be dictated to by my damned conscience.'

'You don't possess such a thing as a conscience, Jarvis,' she contradicted scathingly, too angry to be aware of the danger she was in as she backed away from him. 'It isn't your conscience that made you move out of this room, it was the fear that I might become pregnant again. It wouldn't do for me to have a child, would it? A child would be an unwanted burden in seven months' time when you can legally claim Eldorado and will want to start divorce proceedings.'

'You can think what you damn well please!'

'Stay away from me!' Gina's heart was beating in her throat when she at last began to suspect his intentions. 'Don't you dare touch me!'

Her frightened glance darted about the room, searching for a way of escape, but the antique four-poster was a barrier between her and safety. She ran towards the bed and leapt on to it with the intention of jumping off the other side in her desperate dash for the door, but she never got farther than the bed. The framework of the four-poster shuddered beneath Jarvis's weight when he lunged at her and, despite her efforts to fight him off, he pinned her arms above her head and held her a helpless prisoner against the soft mattress with the punishing pressure of his rock-hard body on hers.

'You asked for this, Gina, and you've provoked me into a mood to say to hell with everything!' His voice was hoarse, and fury mingled with desire in the smouldering eyes that met and held hers. 'I want you, and I'm going to have you!'

'No!' The cry was wrung from her as she writhed beneath him in a futile attempt to escape. 'I refuse to be used as a plaything you can pick up and cast aside whenever it pleases you.'

'Shut up!' he barked savagely, taking one of her hands and thrusting it inside his robe until her soft palm came into contact with the tantalising warmth of his skin and the abrasiveness of his chest hair. 'You want me, I saw it in your eyes when I walked into this room, and don't deny it, Georgina!'

She stilled beneath him, caught in the fatal trap of her own emotions, and her fingers curled against his chest in an involuntary caress that made him mutter something unintelligible before his hard mouth descended on hers with a bruising passion to which she responded with a fierce desire of her own.

After weeks of abstinence their union was stormy and silent, and Gina matched the pace Jarvis had set until they came together in a shattering climax which left them gasping weakly for breath. There was no need to express in words the intensity of their physical need, and when their pounding heartbeats subsided they reached for each other again with a mutual hunger for a deeper satisfaction.

Gina was by nature an early riser, and she felt completely disorientated the following morning when she awoke to find that she had slept until eight-thirty. She was stretching lazily, her mind unwilling to recall what had occurred during the night, when she saw a note propped up against the reading lamp on the bedside cupboard. She sat up in bed with a jolt, her head skipping an anxious beat as she snatched up the note and read it.

'Last night should not have happened, but I'm not going to apologise for it' Jarvis had written in his bold handwriting. *'The time has come, however, for a frank discussion and a decision which might have a drastic effect on our future.'*

She was wide awake now as she read through the letter a second time in the hope of grasping its contents. She agreed that it was time they had a frank discussion, but what decision did they have to make that might have a drastic effect on their future? Was Jarvis implying that he might want to end their marriage? No! He would never do anything to lose Eldorado. Would he?

Gina telephoned his office later that morning. She
had to talk to him; she had to know what he had
been trying to imply in his letter, but Mrs Jackson
told her that he had already left the office and that
would be in court for the remainder of that morning.

Restless and agitated, Gina got into her Alfa and
drove into the city. She might have found something
at Eldorado with which to keep herself occupied, but
the walls seemed to be closing in on her once again,
and she simply had to get out. She wandered along
the city streets, window-shopping and buying a few
unnecessary items as she had done so often during the
past weeks, but when she arrived back at the car with
her parcels, she had made up her mind to pay a visit
to the Supreme Court where Jarvis would be defending
one of his clients. If they were going to have a frank
discussion, then they might as well have it as soon as
possible and not prolong the agony.

After making a few enquiries at the Supreme Court
building Gina was directed to where she would find
her husband, and she quietly entered the packed court-
room to watch Jarvis in action without his knowledge.

A witness had taken the oath before being
questioned by the state attorney and, from what Gina
could gather, the evidence that was put forward was
almost sufficient to send Jarvis's client to prison for a
lengthy period. The witness in the stand was a short,
stocky man with a brash, confident demeanour which
did not falter during the lengthy interrogation. The
State Attorney finally resumed his seat amid the
murmur of excited voices, and during a plea for silence
it was Jarvis who rose imperiously to approach the
witness stand. He looked distinguished and awe-
inspring in his court-room garb, and Gina's heart
missed several beats in a mixture of fear, pride and
pleasure at being able to observe him like this, but, as
the interrogation began, she felt herself shrink inwardly

in sympathy with the witness. Jarvis had become a
dangerous predator, stalking his prey relentlessly and
patiently and, when the opportunity arose, he pounced.
Not once did he raise his voice, but his ruthless, almost
brutally phrased questions had the witness sweating,
stammering, and finally contradicting himself to the
point where no self-respecting jury could possibly
consider his evidence reliable.

This was a side of Jarvis that Gina had encountered
to some extent over the past months. He could be
brutal, ruthless, and deceitful in achieving his objec-
tive, but he could also be gentle and considerate, and
it was the latter on which she preferred to dwell.

The murmur of voices in the court-room rose to a
crescendo when the witness was finally asked to leave
the stand, and at this point in the proceedings it was
decided to call for a recess until two o'clock that
afternoon.

Gina left the court-room as quietly as she had
entered it, but she waited outside the building in the
hope of meeting Jarvis and arranging to have lunch
with him. This was perhaps not the right time, and a
restaurant might not be the ideal place for a personal
discussion, but for some obscure reason she felt it
could not be delayed.

People were streaming out of the building into the
warmth of the wintry sun, and some minutes elapsed
before Jarvis appeared at the entrance. Gina took an
involuntary step in his direction, her hand lifting to
capture his attention, but the next instant she froze.
Lilian Ulrich was at Jarvis's side, her arm linked
intimately and possessively through his, and they were
so engrossed in each other that neither of them noticed
Gina, who was standing a short distance away with a
stricken look on her pale face.

A door slammed inside her and a light went out
somewhere to leave her with the feeling that she had

entered a dark hall of death. This was the end, she
could take no more!

Her feet felt like lead as she walked to where she
had parked the car, and she drove aimlessly through
Johannesburg's busy streets until her mind began to
function on a vaguely constructive level. She found
parking near a telephone booth and, taking a few
coins out of her purse, dialled Harold Ashton's
number.

'I'd like to see Mr Ashton this afternoon,' she told
his secretary moments later. 'It's urgent.'

'Your name, please?'

'Georgina Cain.'

'Just a moment.' There was a brief pause, and Gina
could imagine the woman checking the lawyer's
appointment book. 'Mr Ashton could see you this
afternoon at two-thirty, if that would be convenient
for you.'

'That would be perfect, thank you.'

Gina's eyes were dark pools of anguish in her
unnaturally white face, but her actions were rigidly
controlled as she replaced the receiver. There was only
one course left open to her, and perhaps Harold
Ashton could give her the advice she needed.

She skipped lunch that day. She could not have
eaten even if she had been paid to do so, but neither
could she sit about idly, and she drove aimlessly
through the streets once again until it was time for
her appointment with Harold Ashton. She was ten
minutes early when she finally arrived at his rooms,
and she picked up a magazine to leaf through, but the
articles on the glossy pages did not capture her interest.
She was turning the pages periodically for the sole
purpose of keeping her hands occupied, and she did
not have long to wait before she was called into the
office beyond the panelled door.

Harold Ashton rose behind his desk to study her
curiously and somewhat warily when she entered his
office. 'Please sit down, my dear, and tell me in what
way I may be of service to you.'

Gina seated herself in the chair he had indicated
and she came straight to the point when she faced the
lawyer across his wide, cluttered desk. 'I would very
much like to know the exact conditions stipulated in
that clause which my godmother added to her will.
Would you consider it unethical if I asked you to read
it to me?'

'I don't have Evelyn Cain's will here with me now,
but I'm fully versed as to its contents.' Harold Ashton
looked discomfited as he cleared his throat and fiddled
with the gold pen on his blotter. 'It stated quite
categorically that Jarvis had to marry you as soon as
possible, and that he was to stay married to you for
twelve months in order to inherit Eldorado. During
this time you are both expected to live in the house,
and, should your marriage be dissolved before the
year has expired, the contents of the house must be
sold, and the proceeds used to equip Eldorado as a
children's home.'

Gina felt as if a noose had been tightened about
her throat. 'In other words,' she croaked, 'Jarvis loses
his inheritance if I move out and live elsewhere.'

'That is quite correct.' He eyed her speculatively.
'Do you wish to move out of Eldorado?'

Gina hesitated momentarily, but this, she decided,
was not the time to be evasive. 'Mr Ashton, I simply
can't continue with this marriage as it stands, and you
of all people must understand why. Is there no way
Jarvis could inherit his family home without those
dreadful and intolerable conditions in his mother's
will?'

The lawyer shook his greying head. 'I'm afraid the
only way Jarvis can inherit Eldorado is to comply

with the conditions laid down by Evelyn Cain herself.'

Gina sagged in her chair and pressed the tips of her
fingers against her throbbing aching temples. She had
to think, but she was having difficulty in doing so.
Her mind refused to function beyond this dead-end
information, and a wave of helplessness and despair
washed over her. She had to get away, she had to
think, and she could not do that at Eldorado.

'Is there anything to prevent me from going away
for a couple of weeks?' she finally questioned the
lawyer, and a slow smile spread across Harold Ashton's
lean face.

'There's no mention in Evelyn Cain's will to the
effect that you can't take a brief holiday away from
Eldorado with or without your husband.'

Gina felt a stab of relief so intense that tears filled
her eyes, but she blinked them back, and rose calmly
to shake the lawyer's hand.

'Thank you,' she smiled shakily. 'Thank you very
much for allowing me to take up your valuable time
this afternoon.'

She knew now what she had to do, her immediate
plans were suddenly crystal clear, and she drove back
to Eldorado in a positive if not a lighter, frame of
mind.

She packed a suitcase, and gave the house servants
the necessary instructions before she went into the
study and seated herself at Jarvis's desk. She would
have to leave him a note, but what was she going to
say? What *could* she write except the truth?

'*Dear Jarvis,*' she started the letter in her small, neat
handwriting. She stared hard at those words, and
changed her mind. '*Dear Jarvis*' had a ring of affection
to it which she had no intention of implying, and she
crushed that sheet of paper between her hands before
she threw it into the fire which was burning lustily in
the grate. She drew a clean sheet of paper towards her

and stared at it blindly. What did one write to one's husband under circumstances such as these? Could she explain her reasons for wanting to get away from him without flinging accusations at him?

Jarvis, her pen scraped his name across the sheet of paper after precious seconds had ticked by, *I spoke to Harold Ashton this afternoon, and our discussion led to my hasty decision to return home to my family for a few weeks. I need time to myself to get my life back into perspective, and I can't do this while I'm with you, or at Eldorado. You must know as well as I do that we can't go on the way we are. That's why I strongly suggest we take this time away from each other to think things out, and to decide finally what we're going to do about our marriage.*

Forgive me for leaving without warning, but there was no other way. Gina.

She grimaced when she read what she had written. The letter sounded stilted, but it would have to do, she decided as she slipped the folded sheet of paper into an envelope, and left it on the desk where she knew Jarvis would find it.

A jerky sigh escaped her when she drove away from Eldorado, and she could not decide whether she was experiencing a feeling of relief or a sense of freedom. She had never before felt so dead inside. *You don't have what it takes to hold a man like Jarvis Cain.* Lilian's remark flitted through her mind, and it was followed swiftly with a vision of Jarvis and Lilian leaving the Supreme Court, arm in arm, their heads close together to suggest an intimacy in their conversation. Gina waited for that familiar stab of pain, but it did not materialise. She felt nothing, only a terrible emptiness as if a vacuum had taken the place of what had once been her heart.

She drove on, staring straight ahead of her through the lenses of her dark glasses, and aware of nothing

except an impatience to reach her destination. She had
not telephoned her family to let them know that she
would be coming home for a while, but she had no
doubt that they would make her feel welcome. She
needed the solitude the farm had to offer, but most of
all she needed to surround herself with people whom
she knew and loved.

CHAPTER NINE

THE sun had hovered like a brilliant ball of fire on the horizon before it had dipped behind the distant hills, and its departure had left a chill in the air that made Gina shiver behind the wheel of her Alfa. The cloud-flecked sky had darkened swiftly, and the stars were becoming visible when she turned off on to the gravel road which led towards the farm. The lights were on in the rambling old house, shining out a welcome, and it felt good to be home. She parked the car and, zipping up her fleece-lined jacket to ward off that cold August breeze, took her suitcase out of the boot and went inside.

Her unexpected arrival aroused exclamations of surprise and delight from the men, but Susan studied Gina intently and curiously for several long seconds before she smiled and said, 'It will be nice to have you home again for a while.'

No one questioned her, and if her silence at the dinner table that evening seemed odd, no one said anything. It was a typical reaction, and Gina blessed them for it. They knew she would talk if and when the need arose, but until then they would not pry, and that was how it had always been between them.

The telephone rang shrilly when they were drinking coffee in the lounge where a log fire crackled in the grate, and Clifford got up with a sigh to answer it.

'That was Jarvis on the phone,' her brother enlightened her when he returned to the lounge a few minutes later. 'He wanted to make sure you'd arrived safely.'

As if he really cared! Gina thought cynically when she had recovered from her initial surprise. It was all a sham, this display of husbandly concern, and it sickened her.

'He said to tell you you're not to worry, he would see to everything,' Clifford continued as he resumed his seat in front of the fire. 'And you're to stay as long as you like.'

The latter half of that odd message made humiliating sense. The lengthier her stay on the farm, the more freedom Jarvis would have to come and go from Eldorado as he pleased. It would leave him free to see Lilian as often as he wished without the bother of a suspicious, jealous wife waiting for him at home. She was, however, confused and disturbed by the first half of that message. She was not to worry, he would see to everything. What was it that she was not supposed to worry about? And what was the 'everything' that he would see to? Her mind seemed too tired to think clearly, her thoughts spun in senseless circles, and in the end she could do no more than shrug the matter aside.

The family retired early, as they always did, and Gina went to her old room to discover that a change had taken place since her last visit. The old twin beds had been replaced with a modern double bed and, as a result, she spent a restless night fighting against that seemingly vast, empty space beside her. 'Dammit!' she cursed loudly into the darkness after what had seemed like hours of restless tossing and turning. As much as she hated to admit it, she had become accustomed to sleeping with Jarvis. She had accepted his absence from her bed at Eldorado during the past weeks, but on this occasion it made her shiver with cold and ache with an intense loneliness.

She eventually drifted into a troubled, restless sleep, but she was up before dawn the following morning. She dressed warmly in denims, riding boots, and a long-sleeved blouse under her fleece-lined jacket. She left her room and walked quietly down the passage towards the kitchen to make herself a cup of coffee, but soon discovered that she was not the only one to have risen early.

'You looked so tired last night I thought you would sleep late this morning,' Susan remarked conversationally as she placed two mugs on the table and poured steaming black coffee into them. 'Don't tell me you're missing Jarvis already?'

That was a joke, and she was supposed to laugh, but the best Gina could do was force her lips into the semblance of a smile when she seated herself at the table and helped herself to milk and sugar.

'Something is wrong, isn't it, Gina?' Susan's quietly spoken words intruded on the companionable silence between them, and Gina's hands started to shake before she could open her mouth to protest. 'Oh, don't pretend with me,' Susan forestalled her. 'The men may be too blind to notice, or too polite to mention it, but I'm not.'

Gina's facial muscles went rigid, and her cold, trembling fingers tightened about the mug in search of warmth. 'I don't want to talk about it.'

'Suit yourself, my dear,' Susan agreed amiably, 'but I can be a pretty good listener if you ever feel the need to get something off your chest.'

'I'll remember that,' Gina replied, but at that moment she had neither the desire nor the intention to discuss her problems with anyone. She drained her mug and got up to rinse it out under the tap in the sink. 'I'm going to give Jupiter some exercise, but I'll be back before breakfast.'

'Gina . . . ' Susan's blue eyes were clouded with concern as she hesitated. It was obvious that she had wanted to say something she considered important, but for some reason she changed her mind. 'Take care,' she warned, smiling warmly.

Gina felt her heart contract. She was, at last, among people who cared, and it was like balm on the raw wound inside her. 'Thanks, I shall,' she assured Susan.

Jupiter was in a frisky, impatient mood, and Gina needed every scrap of concentration to control him. They raced across the veld, wild and free, and did not stop until they reached their favourite resting place on the brow of the hill where Gina could watch the sun beyond the hills in the distance. She slackened her hold on the reins, but remained seated in the saddle. Her cheeks were stinging, and her hands ached with the cold, but she was only vaguely aware of this as she stared blindly into the distance.

This was where Jarvis had kissed her for the first time. She could remember her anger at the alien feelings he had aroused, and then there had been his mockery as if he had known exactly what she felt and thought. *Damn him*! Right from the very beginning he had had that uncanny ability to read her like a book. He knew her weaknesses, he knew her strengths, and he knew exactly which strings to pluck, as if she were a violin and he the master violinist. Oh, he was very clever! He had used his expertise with women to enslave her completely until she had been like malleable clay in his hands. He had given up his much cherished freedom to marry her, and he had done all that for Eldorado. Oh, God, what a blind idiot she had been!

The sun had risen to make every frozen drop of dew glisten like a lustrous pearl, but Gina was too deep in thought to notice. It was only when Jupiter

stepped about agitatedly that she became aware of
a watery glow reaching far into the sky on that
wintry morning. Peace and tranquillity reached out
to her, but it did not calm the turbulence inside her.
Resentment and anger had finally asserted themselves, and burned like a fierce fire, cauterising the
hurt to leave her numb again.

There was more than enough to do on the farm to
keep herself occupied, and Gina helped wherever
she could, but she dreaded the long nights when she
lay awake for endless hours while her mind sifted
through the debris of what her life had become. She
had thought she might stay on the farm for two
weeks, but the two weeks drifted into three, and still
she had no clarity in her mind about what she
wanted to do. Jarvis had not telephoned again, and
neither had he written. Gina had been afraid, at
first, that he might decide to drive down for a
weekend, but he had had the good sense to stay
away.
    She sighed tiredly while she checked Jupiter's girth
and pulled herself up into the saddle. It was a warm
afternoon, and the stallion was ready for a gallop
across the veld. She touched his sides lightly with
her heels, and they shot off at their usual mad pace
to leave Solomon shaking his head reprovingly while
he walked from stable to stable to inspect the
remaining horses.
    Gina allowed Jupiter the freedom to choose his
own path, and she allowed her mind an equally free
rein that afternoon. Her resentment and anger had
burnt itself out long ago. The hurt was still there,
but it was being overshadowed by a deep longing
that was growing steadily, which nothing seemed
capable of assuaging. She had constantly shied away
from analysing her feelings during these past weeks,

but the answer came to her now, and it surged forward with a force that defied her to ignore it. She had been almost convinced that she despised Jarvis for what he had done to her, but that was not the truth. She loved him despite the fact that he had married her solely to inherit Eldorado. She loved him for the man she knew him to be beneath that harsh, sometimes ruthless veneer, and she would go on loving him until she drew her last breath.

'Oh, God, what am I going to do?' she groaned, raising her anguished face to the warmth of the winter sun and letting the breeze whip through her hair. 'What do I do, and how will I go on living without him?'

Jupiter laid back his ears at the sound of her voice, but he did not alter his pace, and they were both pleasantly tired when they returned to the stables an hour later.

Susan was in the kitchen checking on the dinner while spooning cereal into her baby's mouth, and she looked up when Gina walked in and slammed the outer door shut behind her. Baby Anthea's wide blue eyes followed every move Gina made as she helped herself to a mug of coffee, but the child's rosy mouth opened wide every time the teaspoon touched her lips. She gurgled contentedly in between each mouthful, and when she had had enough she turned her face away and rubbed her little fist across her nose and mouth.

Gina observed Susan intently when she wiped Anthea's face and hands before placing the baby in her pram, and a familiar stab of envy shot through Gina. The memory of her accident was still vivid, and that sense of loss had never diminished. More than ever now she wanted a child; she wanted Jarvis's child, but she knew she was wishing for the impossible. There was no future for her with Jarvis, and a child would merely consolidate the chains of marriage he despised so much.

What am I going to do? The question stormed once again through Gina's tortured mind, and it was despair that made her turn at last to Susan for the advice she needed so desperately, but she chose her words with infinite care.

'What would you do, Susan, if you discovered that Cliff had married you not for the usual reasons, but because he'd stood to gain something which was of great value to him?'

Susan turned at the sink, her amused expression sobering when she encountered Gina's grave glance. 'You want to know what I'd do if I discovered that Cliff had married me because he'd stood to gain something which was of value to him?' she repeated Gina's query thoughtfully while she wiped her hands on a kitchen towel and poured herself a cup of coffee. 'First of all, I think, I would make very sure of my facts before I did something I might regret for the rest of my life.'

'Let's say you were absolutely sure. What would you do?' Gina persisted, lowering her dark lashes to veil the pain in her eyes.

'I'd take stock of the situation and I'd ask myself how much do I love him,' Susan answered slowly while she added sugar to her coffee and stirred it. 'If my love for my husband was strong enough to overcome that humiliating barrier, then there would always be the hope that I could make him love me in return.'

How much do I love Jarvis? Gina asked herself analytically. *Do I love him enough to overlook that calculated and cold-blooded reason for our marriage? And what do I do about Lilian Ulrich? Do I have the strength and the ability to compete with a woman who appears to have everything he desires most in a woman?*

'Would you consider that you had reason to hope if an old girlfriend of Cliff's suddenly put in an appearance and you knew they were seeing each other frequently?' she asked, torturing herself by turning the knife in her own wound.

'There's always hope, no matter how desperate a situation appears to be, Gina.' Susan's glance mirrored grave concern when she studied Gina's pale, pinched face, and then that familiar teasing smile lurked in her blue eyes. 'You could, of course, try seduction. You're a beautiful woman, and you have a lovely figure. You could wait up for Jarvis one night, but make sure you wear your flimsiest nightie, and don't forget to wear lashings of your most intoxicating perfume.'

Gina tried to think herself into the part of the seductress and found it laughable. She could also imagine Jarvis's look of blank surprise, and the mental image was suddenly quite hilarious.

She started to laugh, and the fact that Susan stood grinning at her with a quizzical look in her eyes seemed to heighten Gina's amusement, making her laugh until the tears rolled down her cheeks.

'If I haven't helped in any way to solve your problems for you, then I've at least succeeded in making you laugh a little,' Susan pointed out somewhat drily when Gina finally managed to control herself.

'Have I been that boorish?' asked Gina, taking a handkerchief out of her jacket pocket to wipe away her tears.

'You've obviously had a lot on your mind, and it isn't always easy to pretend you're happy when you're actually hurting like the very devil inside.'

Gina stared at her sister-in-law, and tears filled
her eyes again, but this time they were not tears of
laughter.

'Thanks, Susan,' she whispered huskily, hugging
her sister-in-law and kissing her briefly on the cheek
before she fled to the privacy of her room.

She sat down heavily on the bed, and the tears
rolled freely down her cheeks until she could taste
their saltiness in her mouth. She drew a shuddering
breath to control herself and to ease the ache in her
throat, but failed and buried her face in her hands
to weep until there were no more tears left to shed.

She wiped her red, swollen eyes with her soggy
handkerchief and blew her nose while she took
careful stock of herself. She felt drained, but also
strangely cleansed, and she knew at last what it was
she wanted most of all. She wanted Jarvis! She
wanted to see him; she wanted to talk to him, and
touch him. It was as simple as that, and she was not
going to let anything or anyone stand in her way
again. She would pack her suitcase and leave in the
morning for Eldorado, and she could only pray for
the opportunity to make Jarvis love her in return.

She pulled off her dusty boots and dropped them
on the floor before she peeled off her equally dusty
denims and shirt. She bathed and changed into fresh
clothes before dinner, and when she joined the rest
of the family around the table that evening, she
knew she had to inform them of her decision.

'I'm going back to Johannesburg, and I'm leaving
directly after breakfast in the morning,' Gina
announced when their dessert had been served, and
for a brief moment there was absolute silence around
the table as three pairs of eyes were focused on her.

'I guess it is about time you went back to your
husband.' Clifford broke the silence with his teasing
remark.

'Yes, I guess it is,' Gina agreed calmly, her glance meeting Susan's briefly and finding understanding mirrored in those clear blue eyes.

'I'm disappointed that Jarvis didn't have the time to come through for a weekend while you were here,' Raymond Osborne complained.

'Jarvis is very busy at the moment, Dad.' Gina formulated an acceptable excuse. 'Perhaps we'll come for a weekend later in the month.'

Her father nodded without speaking, and the trend of the conversation shifted on to safer ground.

Something happened, however, to make Gina's plans go slightly awry. They had barely risen from the table that evening when the telephone rang, and an unexpected shiver, like a premonition, raced along Gina's spine.

'It's for you,' said Susan, placing the receiver in Gina's hand. 'It's a Mr Harold Ashton from Johannesburg.'

Harold Ashton! What did he want? Had something happened to Jarvis while she had been away? Was he hurt? Dying? Oh, please, God, don't let it be anything serious!

'Georgina Cain speaking,' she said into the mouthpiece, her voice calm despite the frightened thudding of her heart against her ribs.

'My apologies for intruding on your holiday, and at this hour of the evening,' Harold Ashton's familiar voice spoke into her ear, 'but I thought you might like to know that Jarvis came to me this afternoon with a request to start divorce proceedings.'

'He did *what*?' Gina's fingers tightened convulsively on the receiver until her knuckles whitened, and an icy coldness invaded her body to drive every drop of blood from her face.

'He wants me to start divorce——'

'Yes, yes, I heard you!' she interrupted him agitatedly. 'But he can't div—he can't do that! He *can't*!'

'Not if he wants to inherit Eldorado,' the lawyer agreed, and the line went oddly silent before he added shrewdly, 'Perhaps there's something you could do to make him change his mind . . . for Eldorado's sake as well as your own?'

Harold Ashton was no fool. Gina was dismayed at this discovery, and she knew that there would be no sense in denying his suspicions. he had guessed that she loved Jarvis, and this was perhaps the main reason why he had telephoned.

'I'll do whatever I can,' she promised abruptly, and that petrifying coldness was still circulating through her veins when she replaced the receiver moments later.

She remained in the hall a few seconds longer to give herself time to regain her composure before she joined her family in the lounge where they sat around the fire which was crackling in the grate.

'There's been a change of plan,' Gina enlightened them without preamble. 'I'm leaving for Johannesburg immediately.'

Their expressions ranged from stunned incredulity to curiosity and concern, and Clifford was once again the first to recover.

'Has there been an accident?' he demanded. 'Is that why you want to rush back so unwisely at this hour of the evening?'

'There's been no accident,' Gina replied with a calmness she was far from experiencing. 'Something important has come up, something I feel needs my immediate attention, and please don't ask me to explain, because I can't.'

'You know I don't like the idea of a woman travelling alone at night,' her father tried to dissuade her, but Gina shook her head adamantly.

'I must leave now,' she insisted quietly, taking a firm stand. 'It's important . . . *very* important.'

Clifford was on the point of raising an objection of his own, but Susan's hand on his arm deterred him, and Raymond Osborne sighed deeply and resignedly when he saw the look of determination that had settled on his daughter's face.

'If it's so important for you to leave now, then I don't suppose any of us have the right to stand in your way,' he said, filling the bowl of his pipe with tobacco and concentrating on lighting it.

Gina did not linger to have coffee with her family. She went to her room to pack her suitcase, and she did so hurriedly in the hope of getting away from the farm while it was still comparatively early. Her beige slacks and matching thick woollen sweater had been warm enough in the house, but knowing how the temperature could drop at night she put on her fleece-lined jacket before going out of the house. Her family hovered around her in silence while she put her suitcase in the boot of the car, and she hugged each one of them in turn.

'I'll give you a call from Eldorado to let you know I've arrived safely,' she promised, and a few minutes later the Alfa's headlights were slicing through the inky darkness ahead of her as she drove carefully along the bumpy farm track towards the main road.

Gina was as impatient and anxious to reach Eldorado as she had been to leave it three weeks ago. She had to see Jarvis; she had to talk to him, and she had to convince him that a divorce would not be the solution to their problems. She would never forgive herself if she was the cause of Jarvis relinquishing his right to his family home. Eldorado belonged in the Cain family; it belonged to Jarvis, and she would do anything to see that it remained that way.

The drive from the farm to Johannesburg had seldom taken more than an hour, but on that particular night it seemed to take an eternity before the familiar city lights beckoned her in the distance. Yet another eternity seemed to elapse before the Alfa sped up Eldorado's long drive, but Gina was suffering from an unexpected attack of nerves when she got out of her car and carried her suitcase up the shallow steps to the front door.

The lights were on in the hall, and her hand was trembling when she inserted her key in the lock and went inside. She paused at the foot of the staircase with its carved wooden balustrade and quietly put down her suitcase to glance about her. Eldorado. It was a beautiful old house that needed to be lived in and laughed in, but Evelyn Cain had foolishly made it a prison from which there would be no escape unless Jarvis forfeited his right to his inheritance, and he had obviously been driven to choose the latter.

No! She could not allow him to go through with this crazy decision to end their marriage. Eldorado belonged to Jarvis, and her own feelings were of no consequence in this absurd and unbearable situation. She loved him, and she knew now that she loved him enough to do anything and everything within her power to see to it that the home Jarvis loved remained in his possession.

Gina's heart was beating so hard and fast it seemed to her that the heavy thuds were echoing throughout the hall, and she placed a trembling hand against her breast in a conscious desire to steady it. Where was Jarvis? Was he at home, or was he perhaps spending the night with Lilian?

A door opened and closed in the silent house, and Gina spun round with a nervous jerk as if someone had unexpectedly cracked a whip directly behind her, but it was Rosie emerging from the kitchen with a tray on which there was a large flask of coffee and a plate of sandwiches. Rosie halted abruptly in her stride when she saw Gina, and her welcoming smile almost split her face in two.

'I'm so glad you're back, Missus Gina.'

'Thank you, Rose.' Gina forced her unwilling lips into an answering smile and she gestured towards the tray in Rosie's hands. 'Is that for Master Jarvis?'

'Yes, Missus Gina,' Rosie answered politely, allowing Gina to take the tray from her. 'The master is in the study.'

'Thank you, Rosie, you may go.'

Rosie scuttled away into the kitchen, and Gina squared her shoulders, bracing herself for this meeting with Jarvis. What was she going to say to him? Dear heaven, she had been too shocked by Harold Ashton's disclosure to formulate a plan of action. Her only thought had been to get to Jarvis as soon as possible to dissuade him from taking a step that she knew he would regret for the rest of his life.

The study door was closed, and Gina felt her nerves knotting painfully at the pit of her stomach. She was scared, there was no other word to explain how she felt at that moment, but she had to go into that study to face Jarvis. She balanced the tray carefully on one hand and, taking a deep, steadying breath, she knocked and went inside.

The study was in darkness except for the soft, warm glow of the fire burning in the grate, and her heart lurched in her breast at the sight of him standing with his back to the door. His hands were gripping the mantelpiece built over the stone fireplace, and his wide shoulders were oddly hunched beneath his grey woollen sweater. She had always admired him for his seemingly inexhaustible vitality and strength, but at that moment he was projecting an unfamiliar image of tiredness and dejection, and Gina's compassionate, loving heart ached for him.

'You can leave the tray on the desk, Rosie, and that will be all for this evening, thank you,' he said without turning, and that husky, weary note in his voice made her want to weep for him.

Her hands were shaking uncontrollably and, afraid she might drop the tray, she placed it quickly on the cluttered desk before she straightened and turned to stare at his formidable back.

'It isn't Rosie,' she corrected him, swallowing convulsively to ease that uncomfortable lump out of her throat, and a wave of shock washed over her when he spun round to face her.

'Gina!'

Her name seemed to be wrung from him in a hoarse, incredulous whisper that made her throat tighten mercilessly when their glances met and held for tense, interminable seconds.

CHAPTER TEN

'GINA!' Jarvis repeated her name in an umfamiliar, husky whisper as if he were attempting to convince himself of her presence in his study. 'What are you doing here?'

His dark hair lay in untidy strands across his broad forehead as an indication that his fingers had, uncharacteristically, combed through it several times, and his steel-grey eyes glittered strangely in a face that was gaunt and oddly white in the dim light of the fire. Concern rose like a tidal wave inside her, and she knew an impulsive desire to rush to his side, but her control did not falter—she dared not let it.

'You appear to be surprised to see me,' she remarked with a calmness that belied the turmoil inside her while he continued to stare at her intently as if she were an apparition instead of a solid reality.

'I had no idea what length of time you intended to stay on the farm, and when I didn't hear from you during these past three weeks I thought——'

'You thought I'd decided to walk out on our marriage agreement?' Gina filled in for him quietly when he broke off in mid-sentence and gestured oddly with his hands.

His mouth tightened into a grim line and, for the second time since knowing Jarvis, she saw him take a packet of cigarettes off the mantelpiece, and light one.

'We have to talk, Georgina,' he announced, inhaling deeply and allowing the smoke to jet from his nostrils to add a devilish touch to his appearance.

'That's why I'm here, Jarvis. I don't——'

'Before you say anything,' he interrupted her brusquely, his eyes narrowing as she took off her fleece-lined jacket and moved closer to the crackling fire in the grate to warm herself, 'I want you to know that I've done exactly as you suggested in that letter you left me. I've been doing a lot of thinking these past weeks, and I've decided that there's only one thing to do.'

'And that is?' Her voice cracked as something close to fear clutched at her throat. Would she be capable of making him change his mind, or would he insist on a divorce and rob her of the opportunity she needed so desperately to win his love?

'I'm going to give you your freedom, Gina.' Harold Ashton had prepared her for this, but Jarvis's words fell like drops of iced water which fed directly into her bloodstream. 'I know it's what you want and, quite frankly, I want it as well.'

Gina's mind told her that the sensible thing to do would be to accept his statement without argument, but her heart was not in agreement. They both had too much to lose if they went ahead and ended their marriage. She tried to read Jarvis's expression, but he turned away from her to stare at the flames leaping high in the grate. He had become cold and unapproachable, his distant manner making them strangers rather than the lovers they had been during the past months. Gina shivered violently despite the warmth emanating from the fire, and the mechanism of her mind started to grind slowly back into circulation.

'You do realise that if you give me my freedom, you will lose Eldorado?' she questioned him tentatively, wondering whether she ought to tell him that Harold Ashton had warned her of his intentions, but she decided against it.

'I'm well aware of the fact that I shall lose Eldorado!' came the harsh reply, and he drew hard on his half-

smoked cigarette before he flung the remainder into
the fire. 'I've spoken to Harold Ashton, and have
instructed him to go ahead and arrange a divorce. It
shouldn't be a long-drawn-out business, since we'll
both agree to it. They'll require our signatures on
paper, and one of us may have to make a brief
appearance in court, but that will be all.'

It all sounded so orderly and so terribly easy, but
nothing, it seemed, would ever dull the pain inside
her. Gina pulled herself together with an effort. She
must not think only of herself. She had to think of
Jarvis, and what he would be deprived of if she agreed
with this decision to terminate their marriage before
the twelve months had expired.

'I don't want a divorce, Jarvis,' she stated firmly,
but inwardly quaking. 'Not yet, anyway,' she added
hastily.

'I beg your pardon?' He turned to stare at her with
an incredulous look on his face, and she could not
withstand the probing intensity of his glance. 'What
did you say?'

'I said I don't want a divorce. Our marriage may
have been perpetrated for all the wrong reasons, and
I may have been hurt and angry many times, but I'm
not going to let you go through with your decision to
divorce me. This house is big enough to accommodate
two people without the need for us to get in each
other's way unnecessarily. You could always pretend
I'm not here, and you could come and go as you
please, but I——' Her mouth felt horribly dry, and
she swallowed nervously. 'I could never take from you
the only thing you've ever really loved.'

The atmosphere was strained almost to breaking
point during the ensuing silence, and Gina lowered
herself into the leather armchair in front of the fire
when her trembling legs would no longer carry her
weight. She raised her glance at length, but the plea

in her eyes was lost on Jarvis while he stared fixedly
beyond her into the shadowy corner of the room.

'I used to love this old house. It was solid and
dependable, it would always be there as my refuge,
and it would never let me down.' He spoke slowly,
and his words sounded faintly slurred as if he was
speaking his thoughts aloud without actually being
aware of it. 'A relationship between a man and a
woman might falter and die as a result of our fickle
emotions, but I used to believe my love for Eldorado
would survive any crisis.'

Gina stared up at him confusedly, incapable of
dragging her eyes from the attractive though gaunt
planes and hollows of his features accentuated by the
glow of the fire. 'Why are you speaking in the past
tense?' she asked.

'Because that *is* the past, Gina. During these past
weeks of soul-searching I've finally allowed myself to
face the truth, and the truth is that Eldorado means
nothing to me without——' He broke off abruptly,
his face hardening into that familiar, impenetrable
mask, and he turned to gesture towards the tray on
the desk. 'Rosie has prepared enough sandwiches to
feed an army, and there's plenty of coffee in the flask,
if you'd like to join me.'

How could he think of eating and drinking at a
moment like this? How could he be so cool and
sensible when she was almost frantic with the desire
to know what lay behind his oddly disjointed statement?

'I'll have a cup of coffee, thank you.' She accepted
his offer with a hint of growing impatience in her
voice.

Jarvis poured coffee into the cup for Gina, and his
own into the mug attached to the flask. Gina's glance
was troubled as she stared at those strong, slender-
fingered hands which had caressed her so often, and

so intimately. She had a feeling that she had missed
something vital, but her mind was temporarily too
numb to find what she was looking for.

'How's the family?' Jarvis questioned her conversationally when he joined her beside the fire with a
sandwich in one hand and his coffee in the other, and
his cold, aloof manner made her want to weep like a
child for something which she could sense was slipping
far beyond her reach.

'They're fine—just fine,' she managed, getting a
mental grip on herself. 'I've just remembered that I
promised to give them a call to let them know I'd
arrived safely.'

Jarvis gestured without speaking towards the telephone on his cluttered desk, and Gina put down her
cup before she rose from her chair to make the call.

It was Susan who answered the telephone, and they
spoke very briefly, but before Gina could ring off,
Susan said: 'Remember, Gina, if everything else fails,
try seduction.'

'I'll remember that,' Gina promised, her soft mouth
curving in a wry smile as she replaced the receiver.

Seduction. She cast a quick glance at Jarvis, and
decided against it. Seduction was not the remedy for
the problem confronting her, and there was absolutely
no point in attempting to seduce a man who held
himself so rigidly aloof from her.

She returned to her chair in front of the fire, and
they lapsed into a conversation of platitudes that made
her want to scream to ease the tension within her. She
wanted to touch him, she wanted her love for him to
flow from her fingertips while it dared not flow from
her lips, and she needed to feel the strength of his
arms about her. But instead they sat facing each other
across a mental chasm, conversing like polite strangers.

'Jarvis . . . I meant what I said about not
divorcing you and allowing you to forfeit your right

to Eldorado.' She attempted to steer the conversation towards the important issues.

'If you don't mind, Georgina, I've had an extremely heavy day and I'm tired.' His cold voice chilled her to the marrow. 'I suggest we go to bed and sleep on it, and it's possible you might feel differently about it in the morning when we resume this discussion.'

'If—if that's what you want,' she agreed reluctantly, but her mind was not ready to retire for the night. She wanted to thrash this matter out between them, she wanted to know where she stood, but Jarvis's manner remained totally forbidding.

Gina picked up her jacket and preceded him out of the study. He switched off the lights in the hall and carried her suitcase up to the master bedroom for her where he placed it at the foot of the magnificent four-poster bed. Their eyes met when he straightened, and Gina trembled expectantly. She willed him silently to touch her and hold her, but he had become as immovable as the wall behind him. For one crazy moment, however, she thought she had glimpsed that familiar flicker of desire in his eyes, but it was gone so swiftly that it was possible she could have imagined it. An invisible barrier had risen between them to make him completely unapproachable, and it aroused her frustration and anger.

'Goodnight, Gina.' his abrupt voice intruded on her thoughts, and she was astounded when he walked out of the room and closed the door firmly behind him.

She heard him entering the room across the passage, and a wave of cold desolation swept through her to leave her shivering as if she had been dumped in a bath of icy water. She had been so close to him moments ago, and yet so far removed that they might have been standing at the opposite ends of the earth. Gina blamed no one but herself for the present situation, and she was blinded by tears when she knelt on

the carpeted floor to fumble with the catches of her
suitcase until they clicked open.

She undressed and went through her usual nightly
ritual before she got into bed, but she could not sleep.
She was shivering with the cold beneath the blankets,
and she had never felt more lonely. Her tormented
mind launched a replay of every word they had said
to each other in the study. It was as if it wanted to
drive that painful sword deeper into her battered soul,
and she encountered again the curious sensation that
she was overlooking something of vital importance.
What was it? The answer continued to elude her, and
her mind stubbornly refused to let the matter rest
there. It deciphered, dissected, and discarded every
fragment of their conversation that evening until she
felt certain she would go mad. On and on it went, for
almost two hours . . . and then, at last, she knew!
She had asked Jarvis why he had spoken in the past
tense, and he had said that it *was* the past. Eldorado
meant nothing to him without . . . Without what?
Or was it *whom*?

Gina sat up in the darkness, and her hands clutched
agitatedly at the sheets. Was it possible that during
these past weeks of soul-searching he had realised that
Lilian meant more to him than Eldorado? Had he
found that not being free to see Lilian whenever he
wished was too high a price to pay? Or could he have
meant . . . Gina went cold and hot alternately as a
result of the trend of her thoughts. She had to know!
It was vitally important! Was it Lilian he loved more
than Eldorado? Or was it . . . herself?

She did not care how late it was, and neither did
she care at that moment whether Jarvis was asleep or
awake. She jumped out of bed without bothering to
switch on the lights and stormed out of Eldorado's
master bedroom and into the room across the passage.

'Jarvis?' His name passed her lips in an anxious cry
as she padded barefoot across the carpeted floor of
the darkened room. The bed creaked beneath her
weight when she knelt beside Jarvis to take him
determinedly by the shoulders. 'Jarvis, are you awake?'
she whispered urgently, shaking him.

'What?' He had not been asleep, she was convinced
of that when he flung out an arm to switch on the
bedside light. The glare hurt her eyes for a moment as
she sat back on her heels to stare into his angry face.
'For God's sake, Gina, what do you want?' he
demanded harshly.

'I want to talk to you! I've *got* to talk to you! You
said that—that Eldorado meant nothing to you
without——' Her mouth felt dry, and she swallowed
nervously while she directed her gaze at his broad
chest with its mat of dark hair. 'Without whom,
Jarvis? Lilian?'

'Lilian?' The blankets slid down to his lean hips as
he raised himself up against the pillows and stared
back at her with a look of incredulous anger in his
steel-grey eyes. 'Lilian's husband left her a wealthy
widow with a business to run, and I was appointed as
her legal adviser.'

'Are you asking me to—to believe you never had
an affair with her?'

'I'm not asking you to believe anything. I'm telling
you that my relationship with Lilian has been purely
business since the day I married you,' he replied in
the cold, distant voice that chilled her. 'The last time
I saw her was more than three weeks ago when I
found her waiting for me in the corridor of the
Supreme Court, and we had lunch together at my
request. I instructed her to appoint someone else as
her legal adviser, and I also made it quite clear to her
that I wanted her out of *my* life, and *yours* in particular.'

'Why—why mine in particular?' asked Gina, not caring if she looked as bewildered as she felt.

'Did you think I wouldn't guess that Lilian had had something to do with that mysterious illness you developed that night when we dined at Vittorio's?' he mocked her derisively. 'I'd seen her leaving the ladies' room a couple of minutes before you came out, and one look at your face had told me that something unpleasant had occurred between the two of you. Then there was that time when she came here to the house to deliver my tie, and she no doubt tried to insinuate that we were having an affair. When I found her waiting at the Supreme Court that day, I thought it a good opportunity to cut my ties with her completely, and when I arrived home that evening you had gone.'

Gina's heart lifted considerably, but now it was her turn to explain. 'I was waiting outside the Supreme Court for you that day. I was hoping we could have lunch together, and I was anxious for us to—to have that discussion you mentioned in the note I found on the bedside cupboard that morning. I couldn't wait for us to sort out the mess we were in, but when I saw you coming out of the building with Lilian I—I'm afraid I thought the worst.' She stared at him anxiously, unaware that the coldness of the night was stealing into her bones, and that she was shivering. 'Jarvis . . . about Eldorado. You couldn't possibly have meant that it—it means nothing to you without—without *me*, could you?'

The air was almost crackling with tension between them during the ensuing silence. A nerve twitched in his jaw, but other than that Jarvis's face remained shuttered and withdrawn as he reached across the bed and offered her his towelling robe. 'Wrap up, or you'll catch your death in that flimsy thing you're wearing.'

'I don't want to wrap up, and I don't care if I catch my death!' she cried in exasperation, thrusting his robe aside, and not caring that she had begun to shake uncontrollably beneath her nightdress as she knelt on the bed and stared at him with an anguished plea in her green eyes. 'Jarvis, I've got to know!'

An agonising silence prevailed, making her feel as if she were hovering precariously on the edge of a steep and dangerous cliff, and an eternity seemed to pass before his mouth twisted in a derisive smile. 'I suspect my fate was sealed almost six years ago when a freckle-faced kid with pigtails fell out of a tree and into my arms.'

Incredulous joy, sharp and sweet, surged through her with every pounding beat of her heart, but the barrier he had erected was still there between them as if he feared that he might be hurt should he tear it down.

'Why didn't you tell me?' she asked unsteadily.

'I didn't know it myself, and when I began to suspect it, I found I was having difficulty coming to terms with the knowledge that I could feel that way about you.' He smiled twistedly, directing his mockery at himself. 'I don't know if you realise it, but it's quite a shock to a man's system when he finds himself confronted with something he'd never believed in before.'

'Oh, Jarvis!' Tears filled her eyes and collected like drops of sparkling dew on her dark lashes before they spilled down her cheeks. 'I've been through a hell of a time trying to sort myself out, but I realised I had to come back to you to tell you that I love you despite everything, and that I was determined to make you love me a little. I was going to leave the farm first thing in the morning, but I received a call from Harold Ashton earlier this evening to tell me that you'd asked him to start divorce proceedings, and that precipitated

my return to Eldorado. I would rather fight Lilian to
the bitter end to get you, but I wasn't going to let you
give up your right to your home.'

'What damn fools we are!' he groaned, reaching out
a hand to brush the tears from her cheeks with tender
fingers. 'It was when you fell down the stairs and lost
the baby that I finally faced up to the fact that I cared
enough to want you to be the mother of my children,
but I'd treated you so badly in the past that my
conscience wouldn't let me come near you until I'd
found a way of convincing you that my feelings were
sincere, and that was why I moved into this room,' he
explained, answering the question which had tormented
her during those long, empty weeks after her accident.
'It also took these three weeks without you to make
me realise, once and for all, that you meant a hell of
a lot more to me than this house, and that I'd gladly
give up Eldorado in the hope of retrieving what I'd
begun to think I'd lost. I'm still prepared to go
through with the divorce if it will convince you of my
feelings for you.'

He would do it too! Gina could see it in his eyes,
and in the determined set of his strong, relentless jaw.
He would relinquish his rightful inheritance to prove
the strength of his love for her, but she shook her
head and gripped his wrist with trembling fingers to
press her quivering lips against his palm in a brief,
tender kiss. 'You don't have to do that, my darling.'

'Come here,' he ordered throatily, pulling her shivering body towards him, and lifting the blankets
invitingly for her to slide into bed beside him.

This was heaven, Gina decided when he held her
tightly in his arms and willed some warmth into her
body with his own. This was where she belonged, and
she was never going to leave again. She clung to him,
breathing in the familiar male smell of him, and she
buried her face briefly against the hollow of his

shoulder before she raised her eager lips to his. They kissed tenderly, but tenderness exploded into a mutual hunger that left them both shaken and breathless with the force of their emotions.

'God knows, I've so much to atone for,' he murmured into her fragrant hair when she moved unashamedly closer to his hard, male body and entangled her legs with his. 'When I saw you at my mother's funeral I knew that I had to see you again, but immediately afterwards I was enlightened as to the contents of her will. I was so furious that I think I went a little crazy, and it was exactly as you once said. I had a notion that you might have had a crush on me when you were a teenager and, taking that into consideration, I decided it would be the easiest thing on earth to make you fall in love with me. I knew you wouldn't marry me any other way, and I cold-bloodedly chose to marry you if that was the only way I could inherit Eldorado, but things didn't quite work out the way I'd planned.'

'Would you have continued with the pretence if I hadn't overheard your conversation with Harold Ashton on our wedding day?' she questioned him, finding no pain now in remembering.

'I don't think I was still pretending at that stage, and that was where my problems started,' he admitted roughly, his arms tightening convulsively about her slim, yielding body. 'My feelings had become involved in a way which I couldn't and *wouldn't* accept, and when you confronted me with what you'd discovered I felt guilty as well as angry at the knowledge that I couldn't deny the fact that I had married you to inherit this house.'

'I was hurt and humiliated, and I know I said a few horrible and regrettable things to you on our wedding night,' she admitted, cringing inwardly at the memory of what had passed between them in that hotel suite.

'I deserved every one of them.' Jarvis laughed shortly, but there was no mirth in the sound. 'I'd treated you abominably, and I should have left you in peace, but something inside me made me use the physical side of our marriage in an attempt to break through that mental barrier you'd erected between us. That didn't work so well either. You drifted further away from me during the weeks and months that followed, and I finally withdrew myself from you completely when you had that accident and my conscience became a punishing factor.' His warm mouth brushed against her eyes and her cheeks before it settled on her lips in a lingering kiss which had the effect of a healing balm. 'I don't mind admitting that it scared the hell out of me when I arrived home three weeks ago and found your letter on the desk in the study,' he continued. 'My first reaction was to drive out to the farm to bring you back by force, if necessary, but that was purely a selfish reaction. I had to give you time to yourself, I owed it to you, and I had to do some thinking of my own. I had to get my priorities in order and, when I finally admitted to myself that you had become the pulse of my existence, I knew there was only one way I could possibly win you back. I had to approach you with honesty, but before I could do that, I had to get rid of that intolerable barrier between us.'

'Eldorado,' she murmured with a trace of bitterness in her voice which she could not disguise.

'Yes, Eldorado,' he repeated grimly, his hands stroking her absently as if to make himself believe that she was actually there with him and not just a figment of his imagination, and her pulse rate quickened with the familiar longing. 'I must admit that my mother was quite a remarkable old woman,' he added mockingly. 'I think she must have known me better than I'd imagined, and it's obvious that she must have seen

something in you to make her believe that we were
meant for each other.'

'Obviously,' Gina agreed, no longer listening to
him, and growing impatient beneath the intimacy of
his absent caresses. 'Don't you think this single bed is
slightly on the uncomfortable side for two?'

She felt his heartbeat quicken beneath her hand. 'Is
that an invitation, Gina?'

'We can't possibly share this bed,' she defended
herself crossly when an embarrassing warmth flooded
her cheeks, 'and if you think I'm going to spend the
night alone in that enormous bed across the passage,
then you're mistaken!'

Jarvis was shaking with silent laughter, but it finally
passed his lips in a low, throaty rumble when he lifted
her out of his bed as if she weighed nothing at all and
carried her across the passage into the master bedroom.
He kicked the door shut behind them, and found his
way towards the bed in darkness. His laughter became
a groan of pleasure when she trailed the tip of her
exploratory tongue along his collarbone and nipped
at his smooth skin with her teeth, and it was her own
hands rather than his that lifted the lacy straps of her
nightdress off her shoulders so that it slithered down
her body to lie on the floor.

The weeks of separation had sharpened their hunger
for each other, and they fell across the bed, their
naked bodies clinging, and the urgency in the touch
of their lips and hands igniting a fire that threatened
to consume them. The knowledge that Jarvis loved
her had given Gina a sense of freedom she had never
experienced before, and she rejoiced in it, her legs
entwining with his as she gave herself to him for the
first time with no fear of humiliation or embarrassment. They had never made love like this before, with
a desire to give as much as they were receiving, and
she would have wished this magical moment to last

for ever, but their need was too intense to prolong the
ultimate pleasure they sought in each other.

The heavy thudding of their hearts seemed to fill
the silent darkness in the aftermath of their lovemaking, and several minutes elapsed before Jarvis
raised himself on one elbow to rest his damp forehead
against Gina's.

'Sweetheart . . .'

'Yes, my darling?' she questioned on a sigh, ecstat-
ically happy and drowsily content for the first time in
their marriage.

'I love you.'

Gina felt her heart lurch with a happiness almost
too painful to bear. She knew how difficult it had been
for Jarvis to say the words she had longed to hear.
They were a direct contradiction of his earlier beliefs,
but he had said them all the same—because it was the
truth, and because he was afraid she might still harbour
a few doubts about him. It hurt to encounter this
uncertainty in the man she loved. He had always been
so confident, and sometimes ruthless in his beliefs,
and she could not bear to think of him in any other
way.

'I know,' she whispered tenderly, drawing him down
into her arms until his dark head rested heavily against
her breast. 'I know you love me, and you know that
I love you, Jarvis. I always have, and I always will. I
tried very hard to put you out of my mind and my
heart during the two years before we met again at
your mother's funeral, but I never quite succeeded,
and that was mainly why I tried to avoid becoming
involved with you again. I knew I wouldn't forget you
so easily a second time, but in the end you won, and
that was why it hurt so much when I discovered the
reason for our marriage.' She felt him move against
her and she combed her fingers lightly through his
hair in an attempt to soothe him. 'I think the worst

part of it all was knowing I was capable of competing against a woman like Lilian, but I knew I couldn't compete against Eldorado.'

Jarvis moved his rough cheek against her breast as if he could no longer tolerate the memory of it all and, when his warm mouth found hers in the darkness, it seemed to shut out everything except the happiness they now shared. They clung to each other with a renewed hunger, and Gina could not suppress the feeling that they were like two people released from a prison erected by Evelyn Cain's foolish, loving fears. This would be a new beginning for them, and the breeze outside seemed to penetrate the walls to whisper throughout the house as if Evelyn in her heavenly home had uttered a contented, triumphant sigh.

Harlequin Presents

Coming Next Month

Available in January wherever paperback books are sold, or through Harlequin Reader Service:

In the U.S.
901 Fuhrmann Blvd.
P.O. Box 1397
Buffalo, N.Y. 14240-1397

In Canada
P.O. Box 603
Fort Erie, Ontario
L2A 5X3

"GIVE YOUR HEART TO HARLEQUIN" SWEEPSTAKES
OFFICIAL RULES
NO PURCHASE NECESSARY TO ENTER OR RECEIVE A PRIZE

1. To enter and join the Preview Service, scratch off the concealment device on all game tickets. This will reveal the values for each Sweepstakes entry number, the number of free books you will receive, and your free bonus gift as part of our Preview Service. If you do not wish to take advantage of our Preview Service, only scratch off the concealment device on game tickets 1-3. To enter, return your entire sheet of tickets.

2. Either way your Sweepstakes numbers will be compared against the list of winning numbers generated at random by computer. In the event that all prizes are not claimed, random drawings will be held from all entries received from all presentations to award all unclaimed prizes. All cash prizes are payable in U.S. funds. This is in addition to any free, surprise or mystery gifts that might be offered. Versions of this Sweepstakes with different prizes may appear in other mailings or at retail outlets by Torstar Ltd. and its affiliates. This presentation offers the following prizes:

(1)	*Grand Prize	$1,000,000 Annuity
(1)	First Prize	$25,000
(2)	Second Prize	$10,000
(5)	Third Prize	$5,000
(10)	Fourth Prize	$1,000
(2,000)	Fifth Prize	$10

. . . *This presentation contains a Grand Prize offering of a $1,000,000 annuity. Winner may elect to receive $25,000 a year for life up to $1,000,000 or $250,000 in one cash payment. Winners selected will receive the prizes offered in the Sweepstakes promotion they receive.

Entrants may cancel Preview Service at any time without cost or obligation (see details in the center insert card).

3. This promotion is being conducted under the supervision of Marden-Kane, an independent judging organization. By entering the Sweepstakes, each entrant accepts and agrees to be bound by these rules and the decisions of the judges which shall be final and binding. Odds of winning in the random drawing are dependent upon the total number of entries received. Taxes, if any, are the sole responsibility of the winners. Prizes are nontransferable. All entries must be received by March 31, 1988. The drawing will take place on April 30, 1988 at the offices of Marden-Kane, Lake Success, New York.

4. This offer is open to residents of the U.S., Great Britain and Canada, 18 years or older except employees of Torstar Ltd., its affiliates, subsidiaries, Marden-Kane and all other agencies and persons connected with conducting this Sweepstakes. All Federal, State and local laws apply. Void wherever prohibited or restricted by law.

5. Winners will be notified by mail and may be required to execute an affidavit of eligibility and release which must be returned within 14 days after notification. Canadian winners will be required to answer a skill testing question. Winners consent to the use of their name, photograph and/or likeness for advertising and publicity in conjunction with this and similar promotions without additional compensation. One prize per family or household.

6. For a list of our most current prize winners, send a stamped, self-addressed envelope to: WINNERS LIST c/o MARDEN-KANE, P.O. BOX 701, SAYREVILLE, N.J. 08872.

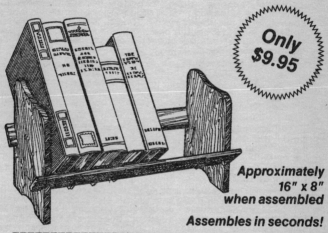